Barbara,
   Best wishes for 21

                Rodney.

WHY?

by Rodney Marshall

Cover photo: Falling Autumn Leaf –
courtesy of *Getty Images* (*iStock.*)

Why? is a work of fiction. Names, characters, businesses, places, events and incidents are either the products of the author's imagination or used in a fictitious manner.

© 2016 Rodney Marshall. All rights reserved.

About the author:

Rodney Marshall is a former lecturer in Victorian literature at Exeter University. The son of television and film script writer Roger Marshall, he has published *Wolf's Hook*, four intertwined short stories based on real life Nazi war crimes; *Blurred Boundaries*, the first full-length study of Ian Rankin's *Inspector Rebus* novels; in addition, he has written or edited twelve books on British television. He lives in Suffolk and South West France.

Books published as sole writer:

Blurred Boundaries: Rankin's Rebus
Wolf's Hook
Subversive Champagne: Beyond Genre in The Avengers
Adventure & Comic Strip: Exploring Tara King's The Avengers
Making It New? A reappraisal of The New Avengers
Blake's 7: A Critical Guide to Series 1-4
Travelling Man: A Critical Guide to the 1980s drama series

As co-writer:

Man in a Suitcase: ITC-land Volume 1

As editor:

Bright Horizons: The Monochrome World of Emma Peel
Mrs. Peel, We're Needed: The Technicolor World of Emma Peel
Anticlockwise: The Psychedelic World of Tara King
Avengerland Regained: The New Avengers
Avengerland Revisited: A Thematic Guide
The Hour That Never Was: Classic British Television Drama

'Suicide is complex. It usually occurs gradually, progressing from suicidal thoughts, to planning, to attempting suicide and finally dying by suicide.'
(International Association for Suicide Prevention)

ONE

Devil's Dyke. From the vertiginous hills there were spectacular views far beyond the deep valley: the chalk escarpments of the South Downs, the woodland and farms of the Weald...on a clear day you could see the Isle of Wight. The irony of the location was not lost on Kate. Was her choice accidental? Of course not. She had chosen to spend her final moments in a place of significance to her. When she was a little girl, Dad had brought her here with Peter. With its permanent squadron of multi-coloured hang-gliders, it had been the scene of happy rambles, games of hide & seek, and family picnics. Mum had often been absent, busy with her latest exhibition. As she always reminded them, it was easier for their father. After all, university lecturers spent most of the year 'on holiday'. Even then, aged what? – seven or eight, perhaps? – she had been acutely aware of the family tensions. She hadn't always helped matters. She recalled her brother asleep in the wild grass after a long, leisurely lunch, Dad probably busy admiring the landscape. She'd stretched out to grab a grape from the hamper, squeezed the juice onto him, knowing how he would react to the sticky, gooed ear when he awoke. Positively looking forward to it. She smiled at the memory. All good-natured Peter had ever wanted was to be allowed to play with her, yet she had always felt the need to wind him up. Still, she loved him dearly and knew how much she would miss him, if that was indeed possible.

Below her she could make out a couple of transparent orbs rolling downhill. They reminded her of Hetty, her pet hamster. Devil's Dyke had been about kite flying when her father was a kid, now it was zorbing. Fashions changed, but the desire to invent fun new forms of entertainment didn't.

Eighteen months ago, Kate had instinctively chosen this place for a first year essay at university. The Dyke had once been home to hunter gatherers, then Stone Age farmers; later, an Iron Age hillfort taking advantage of the commanding views and steep terrain. More recently, it was transformed into a late-Victorian pleasure dome. She had pored over grainy photographs of the Steep Grade railway, cable car and the single-track train line which had brought thirty thousand excited visitors inland to enjoy the Dyke's fairground, bandstands and observatory on a Whit Monday in the 1890s. Each period was a vanished age which she had explored with fascination. While writing her essay, she had enjoyed one of her moments of fancy, imagining time swirling around like mist, Stone Age people peering quizzically at the Victorian day tourists.

Even her own childhood memories here were from a vanished age. Was she remembering the family outings and picnics with rose-tinted glasses? Had the sun always been shining? Were they really happier times? She was convinced that they had been. She hadn't had a care in the world. Dad was always relaxed up here and any marital problems were left behind as soon as they boarded the train at Clapham Junction.

She had still felt relatively carefree when she began her Liberal Arts degree at King's College, London University. The independence of student halls, but with Mum a short Tube ride away for home-cooked Sunday lunches and a working washing machine. She had been looking forward to three years digging up the past, without getting her hands dirty, unlike Peter who had decided on an Archaeology degree in Bristol. She had missed Dad since his move to Singapore ten years ago, but – if she was being honest – a little less each year. She wasn't 'Daddy's girl' anymore and last year she hadn't felt the need to visit him out there. Well, that was half the story. Nevertheless, a trip was pencilled in for Easter, Singapore Airlines 'Premium Economy' ticket booked. Dad reckoned that it would provide 'cultural background' for her extended research project on Joseph Conrad's early sea novels. It was a project she wouldn't be writing. A trip she wouldn't be making. She hoped that he would forgive her.

No tears, just a final question entering her mind. Ending it all here, what kind of a message was she sending out?

****

David Jennings's Samsung Galaxy 5 was vibrating in his shirt pocket. He ignored it. Despite the fact that it was almost midnight, the other people in the lift were busy texting or scrolling. He never felt the compulsion to do either. The phone had been a Christmas present from his son, Peter, passed to him with the dry comment, "Welcome to the real world, Dad." He charged it and carried it daily out of a sense of duty, like a pet which had been forced on him and which he now felt obliged to look after.

The apartment block, off the busy Orchard Road, had been a state-of-the-art building back in the mid-1980s. Nowadays it was beginning to show its age and – given the speed with which the Singapore skyline altered – would probably soon be replaced by a more striking glass and chrome skyscraper. Either way, it didn't bother Jennings. His apartment was more shell than home. The spare bedroom was rarely used as such, and was currently full of boxes crammed with books. The galley kitchen was in showroom condition, not because he was house-proud but because he rarely cooked, either for himself or for guests. You didn't need to when you had the retail and entertainment hub of the city on your doorstep. It was hard to believe that – in the not too distant past – this busy concrete jungle had led to fruit orchards and gambier, nutmeg and pepper plantations. Once upon a time, pre-Empire builders, the entire island had been a tropical rainforest, for goodness sake.

Despite never quite feeling that he belonged there, Jennings enjoyed the city. It was vibrant and lively, yet also clean and safe. The public transport worked efficiently. It was everything England wasn't. He also liked the colonial roots. Not because he took any pride in the sense of a British Empire. No, as a Professor who specialised in the works of Joseph Conrad, he simply took comfort from places like the Raffles Hotel where his hero had stayed. He liked that sense of the past still being tangible.

As he entered the narrow hallway of his apartment the phone was vibrating again. Pulling it out of his breast pocket, he recognised the number: his ex-wife. A text message: 'Please ring me as soon as you receive this. Anne.' A strange memory hit him. How much she had disliked Conrad's writing: 'Stilted use of the English language'. She had never understood Jennings's fascination – okay, obsession – with this strange Polish man who came to both the British seashore and the English language as a foreigner and was able to look inside as a curious outsider, writing in such a unique style. He recalled a number of wine-fuelled, heated arguments about various dead writers and artists. Kate had understood Conrad, of course, but their 'collusion' – as Anne called it – had simply made matters worse.

TWO

The air hostess was asking him if he wanted tea or coffee, but all he could hear was Anne's words – 'Kate...dead body...found by a walker in the grass' – and then her sobbing on the phone which he had been holding in front of him on loudspeaker. Words and distress echoing and bouncing from across the world. Anne had been calling from the Brighton mortuary. She had just identified their daughter's body. Didn't want to ring until she was absolutely sure. Twice she had told him that it *was* Kate lying there. Then Marcus had taken over, something about 'no other details yet known'.

The earliest flight he had been able to get from Changi had been the 12:35, landing in London at 19:05, although in body clock terms it would be two the following morning. Jennings sensed that he should have been feeling numb, but instead his mind was whirring. There had been a horrible mistake. The body which had been discovered on Devil's Dyke – of all places – couldn't be Kate's. Anne must have panicked when she identified the corpse. It belonged to someone else.

He knew that she had an important extended essay to hand in that week. Something about African literary voices? Besides, what could she have been doing there? And at such a bleak time of the year? No, there had been some horrendous mistake. He was ready to pass the grief onto someone else. The hope felt hollow, though, even as he gripped hold of it.

He hired a Mini at Heathrow and headed towards Brighton. As a child it had been his holiday paradise: the pier, the shingle beach, the Lanes and, yes, Devil's Dyke. Anne and her second husband, Marcus, were meeting him at the Old Ship. However, first he had an appointment with a police officer at the borough mortuary on

Lewes Road. He had checked on the internet and noted that it was close to the university and Albion's new football ground.

When he arrived he found an unlikely-looking building. He had imagined grey Victorian brick but it was a long, single-storey construction, half-bungalow and half extended wigwam. A young woman inside ushered him towards the Chapel of Rest. A tall, stocky man with cropped grey hair was standing awkwardly outside the entrance. He held out a farmer's hand and shook Jennings's with a sympathetic warmth. The woman cleared her throat and informed him:

"Mr. – sorry, *Dr*. Jennings, you don't need to formally identify the deceased. Mrs. Johnson's already done that. The post-mortem examination will be taking place tomorrow morning. However, you can stay here with your daughter in the Chapel of Rest. We will have to remain with you, though."

Jennings wasn't listening. He was watching the handle turn as the police officer opened the door. There was something surreal or dreamlike about the whole experience, almost as if he had borrowed someone else's body and was standing in it.

****

Anne and Marcus were waiting for him in the hotel's restaurant. There were views of the lamp-lit Brighton promenade from the large windows but neither of them was looking, or eating. Anne had dark bags under her eyes and Marcus' were bloodshot bleary. As Jennings approached them, Marcus Johnson stood up to shake his hand and gestured towards the empty seat. Anne had barely registered his presence.

"Cognac?" Jennings nodded silently, suddenly aware that they were the only guests in the large dining room. Looking at his watch this was hardly surprising: it was one o'clock in the morning. A Hispanic-looking young man, who was wiping glasses at the bar, nodded at Mr. Johnson, as if he too was part of the silently agreed silence. He brought over three large Cognacs on a tray, scooping up the empty ones in the self-same movement. Finally, Anne looked up.

"You've seen her, then?" A single image from the mortuary – how thin she was, almost anorexic. Jennings blinked the picture away, said nothing about it.

"I thought it would be someone else."

"For God's sake, David!" Anne was shaking. Marcus laid a hand gently on his wife's shoulder.

"We *all* wanted it to be someone else. It feels like a nightmare. I've thought of Kate as my own daughter since she was ten years old. She was a wonderful person."

"Please don't talk about her in the past tense." There was an awkward silence. "Where's Peter?"

"He's on a dig in mid-Wales. No reception. We're not telling him over the phone anyway. Marcus and I were planning on driving over there first thing tomorrow. Of course you can come with us. Did you meet DI Miles?"

"Yes." Jennings recalled the warmth of the handshake. A kind gesture in a cruel world. "He told me that – subject to the post-mortem findings – they're convinced that Kate killed herself. I can't accept that. It's ridiculous. That's not Kate. She loved life. She had places she wanted to visit, thousands of books to read." Anne and Marcus said nothing. "Why would she choose death?"

"David, don't you think we've being asking ourselves the same bloody thing? Over and over. Ever since –". Anne's voice trailed away. Marcus picked up the thread. "We gave her all the support – emotional and financial – that we could, David. She had her independence but she still had her bedroom at home. She had everything she needed." The three of them simultaneously caught each other's eyes, sharing the absurdity of the comment. If she'd had everything she needed, wanted, then why take her own life on a bleak midwinter hillside?

DI Miles had earlier told Jennings that he too was the father of a twenty year old. He had shared his bewilderment. "We've raised a generation of strangers." The words had stuck, despite his trance-like state in the mortuary.

Standing up, he realised how tired he was. His eyelids felt puffy, the veins pulsating. He was bewildered, shocked and angry all at once, but he needed to shut his eyes more than anything else. The barman was polishing the optics, probably waiting to go to bed himself. "We all need some sleep," Jennings added, in place of goodnight.

THREE

David Jennings woke to the sight of his own dribble on the pillow. It took him a split-second to register where he was; a moment longer to remember that Kate was dead. It was as if the whole world had changed and he was seeing its harsh new reality for the first time.

Jennings had stayed at the Old Ship many times before: a number of university conferences, a book launch, even a romantic weekend long before he and Anne were married. A sudden, ridiculous thought: he could never stay here again. It felt more like a luxury funeral parlour than a hotel. His phone vibrated on the bedside table. Another message from Anne: 'Peter knows. Bloody *Twitter*. Meeting us at the Coroner's office.' Shit. So much for no reception. Peter would be as devastated as anyone. Perhaps even more so. Kate wasn't simply his big sister; she was his closest friend, confidante, soul mate. He would have died in her place, given the choice.

The post-mortem would be starting about now. Jennings had a friend in Singapore whose wife was a pathologist. The subject had been discussed over dinner one evening. He had found it fascinating, in a macabre, detached way. Now the full, visceral nature of the surgical procedure hit him. Scalpel, incision, dissection...even the words felt harsh, intrusive. He knew that Kate would be left with marks which resembled bruises. DI Miles had warned him that viewing a body after the post-mortem could be 'distressing'. What could be worse than the last thirty-six hours? Jennings's phone vibrated again. He didn't recognise the number but answered anyway.

****

DI Miles greeted him downstairs in the lobby. The hotel had put aside a private room for them to chat in. Jennings had taken an instant liking to him. He avoided professional jargon such as 'the deceased'. He spoke as one human being to another. They shared common ground, but there was, of course, a divide as well. One of them had a twenty year old daughter who was alive and well, as opposed to lying dead on a mortuary slab.

Miles reminded him gently that death leads to a chain reaction: police to coroner, coroner to pathologist, then back to coroner.

"There *will* be an inquest?" Jennings instinctively knew this was important to him. His mind was spilling over with questions; he needed answers. Graham Miles nodded.

"I'm fairly sure that the post-mortem will confirm that your daughter's death was self-inflicted. You need to be able to accept that she took her own life, Dr. Jennings."

"David, please." Miles smiled, accepting the change in formalities.

"Suicide – and I'm not saying that this is what it was – counts as an unnatural death. The inquest – " Jennings felt compelled to interrupt him.

"I don't understand. Are you saying that it might *not* have been suicide?" His mind was whirring.

"The coroner will need to decide if Kate had the intention to die."

Jennings could not accept that his daughter had intentionally pulled the plug on her young life. Had it been a cry for help? DI Miles explained that witnesses would be called: the police officer who was first on the scene, the pathologist, Kate's flat mates, and her university tutor perhaps. Jennings, Anne, Peter and Marcus would all be given 'proper interest' status and would be able to ask questions. Jennings suggested that it sounded like a law court.

"It is, David. The only difference is that there is no prosecution or defence, no hunting out someone responsible for the death. There isn't usually a jury either. Oh, and I should have added that you can only ask questions relating to the medical cause and circumstances of the death." The two men met each other's eyes, two fathers who knew that the questions Jennings would want to ask would be very different ones. He wanted to reach out and open his daughter's black box, look inside to read what had gone wrong. Now he realised that he didn't even have the right to quiz any of those who had been closest to her in the last few days, weeks, months. He only wanted to ask one fundamental question: WHY?

FOUR

The coroner had given permission for Kate's burial or cremation to take place. It was to be a private, family-only ceremony. Peter had surprised both his parents by announcing that his sister had talked about wanting a 'natural burial'. She had even told him where – Woodland Valley in Woodingdean, on the edge of Brighton, overlooking the sea and downs. He scrolled through pictures on his phone: a biodegradable seagrass coffin which resembled an oversized picnic hamper; a grassed valley which looked nothing like a traditional cemetery. Apparently there was a huge demand nowadays for ecological funerals. He'd asked Peter when and why they had been discussing death. His son, fighting back tears, shook his head, reading between the lines as he always had been able to.

"Dad, it was a perfectly normal, perfectly natural conversation."

"Normal? You're nineteen and twenty for God's sake!" Peter blushed. Jennings wanted to take back his words, his snarl, his thoughtless reaction. Christ! He knew how sensitive his son was, always had been. He hadn't meant to upset him even more, but had managed to do so, nevertheless. He bit his tongue, waiting for Peter to continue.

"We were talking about one of our favourite books. Milan Kundera's *The Unbearable Lightness of Being*. You remember when Sabina moves to Paris and attends a funeral in Montparnasse? By chance." Jennings nodded. He remembered. It was a book he faithfully re-read almost every year. "The heavy gravestone horrifies her. It feels as if the mourners are telling the dead person that they don't want him coming back. Kate said that when she was dead she didn't want to be weighed down. She wanted to be free to soar." Yes, that sounded like Kate. "It was about a year ago. We were in the Student Union bar in London. She was on great form.

We searched the internet. Both chose a coffin and location we liked."

Hadn't *he* spent hours as a teenager wandering through cemeteries, reading the inscriptions? That, arguably, had been far weirder. Both his children shared his taste in literature and, when he thought of their favourite writers, which of them weren't obsessed with death? Dickens, Conrad, Kundera, Rankin…Others, like Woolf and Plath, had killed themselves, their writings full of warnings or fore-echoes if you wanted to find them. It didn't mean that all their readers were on a suicide mission, did it?

****

The inquest failed to bring forth any major revelations. Kate's GP confirmed that he was not aware of any mental disorders. Her flat mates were both mature students, studying different courses. Neither one had noticed anything which could explain why Kate might have taken her own life. She wasn't exactly a party animal. No boyfriend that they knew of. Tended to stay in her room. But neither had she seemed depressed. The three weren't close friends. You could see it in the way that the two women spoke. Not cold, or uncaring exactly, but not emotionally involved.

Jennings vaguely recalled Kate selecting the garden flat because it was close to the lecture hall and had outside space, choosing her fellow students because they were quiet and wanted to study. The only surprise was when the one told the coroner that Kate was vegan and didn't drink. Vegan? Lentils and nut roasts? She had always loved her meat and cheese: *confit de canard*, *chèvre chaud*. Anne told him that it was a "typical student thing. It wouldn't have lasted." Perhaps that explained her weight loss; she had looked so frail, emaciated lying there in the mortuary. Picturing the last time he had seen her – would ever see her – Jennings found himself recalling Graham Miles' comment about 'strangers'. How well did he really know her? He and Anne had separated when Kate was ten. She'd grown up without him. It was Marcus who had dealt with the day-to-day experience of living with teenage hormones and other family tensions, while Jennings had been lecturing about textual conflict in dead writers. As Anne had frequently observed, it was fine turning up for birthdays and Christmases armed with presents, but the minute he had left the UK he had forfeited the right to 'interfere', to play a formative role in their children's lives. End of sermon. There was justification in the charge. Outwardly he would probably deny 'abandoning' his own children. Privately, he acknowledged that it was true. And in Kate's case, it was now too late for him to make up for lost time.

Kate's course tutor had spoken briefly at the inquest, saying that she always attended the weekly seminars and had been expected to achieve at least a 'lower second' degree. Jennings had found this odd, baffling. Surely the professor was underplaying Kate's potential? When they had last seen each other, Kate had been hopeful of 'scraping' a First, was keen to take a Masters and begin to climb the slippery slope into academia. She had laughed when her father pointed out that it would be as much about arse-licking the right people as adding letters after her name.

The coroner had decided on an Open Verdict. In his mind there was no doubt that Kate had voluntarily taken a cocktail of pills and alcohol. Had she known they would be lethal? With no obvious tell-tale signs of why she would want to end her young life, he was not totally satisfied that she had intended to kill herself. In summing up he commented:

"It seems inexplicable that a highly educated, ambitious young woman with a loving family and genuine passions should find – in her despair – NO PLACE TO GO."

The phrase burned itself into Jennings's mind. For him, neither the burial nor the inquest had brought any sense of closure. The Open Verdict had mildly surprised Anne and Marcus. They had both been deeply affected by Kate's death, particularly his ex-wife, but he sensed that they needed to move on. Well, he wasn't ready to and the coroner's decision had merely acted as a spur. Was he looking for a scapegoat? Someone or something to salve his conscience? Quite possibly. However, he hoped that his desire to uncover the truth also went beyond that.

FIVE

David Jennings had walked uphill to the pub twice before realising that this *was* where they were meeting. Graham Miles had said 'The Pedestrian Arms, Foundry Street', clearly forgetting that it had been renamed The Foundry some years ago. A friendly-looking man, standing outside smoking, had put him right. Why hadn't he asked him the first time? Well, you could take the man out of England, but you couldn't take the ridiculously reserved nature out of people like Jennings. No fuss please, we're British.

It was mid-evening quiet and, once installed by the roaring open fire, they laughed about the mistake.

"It's still the Pedestrian as far as I'm concerned. Belonged to the same family for over a hundred years. The Hazelgroves. Used to drink in here when I was a young PC. It was a time warp – no music, no juke box, no fruit machines. A proper pub. Mind you, if a test match was on the television, the landlord was glued to it. Only time it was ever turned on. You ended up dying of thirst or serving yourself. Not sure what old Henry would have made of his boozer offering an extensive wine list." Miles paused, sipping his pint, and then gave Jennings what could only be described as a frank stare. "You're still here, then?"

"Brighton, or the UK?" Miles' gesture suggested that his question referred to either, or both. "You're not about to give me the Sheriff 'get out of town' act?"

"Not a bit of it. But I told you at the time, if you wanted to ask questions, you should have hired a solicitor before the inquest."

"I know. But I wasn't thinking straight. I felt...raw."

"And now is the right time to...dig?"

"I feel… hollow…exhausted…but my mind's a bit…clearer. More lucid, maybe. I need to find out why my daughter – with a lifetime of plans and projects to fulfil – would simply throw it all away."

"And you think the answer is here? In Brighton?"

"No. Not necessarily. But it'll do as a base. Not too far from my son in Bristol. Easy to pop up to London."

"What about your job? Hong Kong is it?"

"Singapore. The university has given me 'compassionate leave'. Besides, I'm due a term's sabbatical."

"Holiday?"

"Well, I'm meant to be writing a book."

"What about?"

"I don't want to bore you."

"Then don't. Get on with the story – what's the book about?"

"*Man in a Suitcase.*" Miles' face was blank. "It was a 1960s television drama."

"I've never heard of it."

"Well, that's my point, really. Or one of them. Mid-sixties, people wanted glamour, fantasy: 'out there' plots, heroines in leather, balletic fights. McGill lived in seedy flats, worked for equally seedy clients. The action was real, the endings were downbeat. Viewers weren't ready for it. They wanted popcorn TV."

"So McGill was what – a private detective?"

"Yes. Ex-American Intelligence. Framed and forced to resign."

"Innocent? I've heard that a few times, without turning on the telly."

"I'm sure you have. But McGill is, though. And despite the sleazy world he is forced to work in, he maintains his integrity. He demands the truth."

"Are we still talking about McGill?" Graham Miles winked; David Jennings smiled. He was almost relaxed. He was happy to be there chatting to someone he respected, someone he liked. For the first time in a week, if only for a few precious moments, he could genuinely say that it felt good to be alive. How could his daughter have felt so differently?

****

Jennings had swapped the Old Ship for an out of season holiday let, a studio flat in Hove. The estate agent who had typed up the particulars merited a place on a post-graduate Creative Writing course. More than that, he'd breeze through it with a distinction. The 'sea views' required you to stand on tiptoe at the kitchenette sink. The 'practical shower room' could have given an inmate at Wormwood Scrubs cabin fever. Still, he guessed that holidaymakers wouldn't care. They'd spend the day shopping in the Lanes or at the beach, bringing back shingle in their sandals and sticky rock in their pockets, ready for sleep. The seaside did that to you, it was something to do with the sound of the waves.

His evening with Graham Miles had ended with the DI giving him a piece of advice and a card. The advice was to tread carefully. He might unearth nothing, but then again he might stir up a veritable hornets' nest. The card belonged to an ex-solicitor Miles knew, Sam Gibb, who worked out of a small office near the train station as an inquiry agent. "Sam's reasonably cheap, sometimes cheerful, and not afraid to ask awkward questions". The recommendation came with a warning though: "If Sam thinks you're barking up the wrong tree you'll be told. In no uncertain terms."

Jennings had left his phone charging in the flat. There were three text messages waiting for him. Anne and Marcus were inviting him to dinner on Monday. It would be an awkward evening, but he wanted to ask them a few questions – face to face – and needed to see Kate's room. Peter, who was inviting himself for the weekend. It would be great to spend some time with him, although it would test the agent's description of the studio's 'surprisingly roomy' interior. Finally, Graham Miles: 'Good to meet up. You know that I can't assist you. Not officially. But feel free to ring me if you want to bend my ear. And don't forget to contact Sam.' Jennings added Gibb's number to his contacts, before crashing out on the bed. With the sash window lowered, he fell asleep to the sound of the waves, an audio feature which had, somewhat surprisingly, been missed by the imaginative agent.

SIX

Peter's train from Temple Meads was due in at 15:27. With no direct route, he was having to go via London and cross the capital from Paddington to Victoria. Jennings had been tempted to tell him to hire a car instead; he would have happily paid for it. However, he had stopped himself. He was ashamed to admit that he couldn't remember if his son had passed his driving test or not, another reminder of how distant a dad he had become.

Sam Gibb's office was above a small convenience store on the main thoroughfare between Hove and Brighton. It had a separate front door which he was buzzed through. The steep, carpeted staircase had seen better days. With a single bare bulb on the landing it was hard to tell what shade of brown it had originally been.

A short blonde lady in a tweed suit took his coat and asked him to take a seat. Jennings guessed that she was probably early forties but he was lousy with ages. She might have been ten years younger. The office had bare, un-sanded floorboards and patterned wallpaper which was either retro or genuine 1970s. A small fridge hummed in the corner next to a sink and microwave. When she sat down on the opposite side of the desk Jennings realised that Miles had tricked him. No, that wasn't strictly speaking true. The DI had allowed Jennings to make the assumption that Sam was a man. Gibb raised her eyebrows, inviting him to open the conversation.

"I was expecting something...different," he offered feebly.

"Something, or someone?"

"Well, both, if you want me to be honest."

"If you're not, we won't get very far." She smiled, while Jennings nodded in agreement. She drew breath, dramatically, before continuing. "I used to be a solicitor in Hove, actually. Plush offices, carpets thick enough to dive into, fresh coffee and croissants for clients. Why not? They were paying handsomely for it all and expected to be able to see that. At their leisure. Here, my clients are less interested in veneer. They're in a hurry and want to see their fee spent on shoe leather. If my office was too comfy they might picture me tucked up here in the warmth, rather than out on the cold open road, searching for answers." It sounded like a rehearsed speech, one which had been delivered to numerous, sceptical clients. To be honest, Jennings wasn't bothered by her gender. He only wanted to know whether she was any good. Whether she cared.

"Fair enough. I suppose I've read too many hard-boiled detective novels."

"I can wear a trench-coat with a cigarette drooling from the corner of my mouth if you want, but I'm not a private eye. I'm an inquiry agent."

"What's the difference?"

"For some, semantics. For me, I want to be clear what I *don't* do – blackmail, subterfuge, fraud etcetera. If I believe a client then I'll make inquiries for them, poke my nose over the parapet, as it were. If I believe *in* them, then I may go a step further."

"Crossing no man's land?"

"Meaning that I might introduce you to my little network of contacts, take one or two calculated risks, use a bit of 'sharp practice'. I won't break the law, but I still do some freelance work for the coroner's office and I have been known to namedrop in a search for answers if I think someone is holding back on me. Which they usually are."

"I'd like to hire you."

"Hold on a minute, buster! I haven't said the magic word yet."

"Belief?" Sam offered him brief, silent applause. "What do you want to know?"

"Graham told me that your daughter took her own life."

"Yes...You didn't use that word: *commit*."

"It hasn't been a crime since 1961. Besides, I find it deeply offensive. Talking of which, I need to ask you some difficult questions. Are you prepared to answer them? Honestly and frankly?" Jennings nodded. "Do you accept that your daughter killed herself?"

"Yes."

"That she *intended* to kill herself?"

"I don't want to...but I think I have to accept that it is a possibility... Maybe a probability. Kate was never someone who asked...cried out for help. She was always self-sufficient, in every sense. She believed that you either put your heart and soul into something, or else it wasn't worth it. She used to quote Alexander Pope: 'A little learning is a dangerous thing.'"

"Drink deep, or taste not the Pierian spring." It was Jennings's turn to offer the mimed applause. "In that case, I presume that there is only one question you want answered." Jennings nodded again. "You want to know why?"

"I *need* to know! I *need* to understand!"

"Then you have to understand something else first. It may be that only one person knows. And she can't answer you." Jennings felt tears rising. Sam Gibb most have sensed them too. "However, I do think that is unlikely. But if someone does know, or can at least shed some light, then your problem – *our* first problem, is trying to work out *who*."

"You said *first* problem."

"The second is convincing them to 'confess'." Gibb noted Jennings's quizzical look. "I'm speaking hypothetically now, of course. Imagine that you knew, or sensed even, that someone was feeling suicidal, and you did nothing about it. How would you feel when you found out that they had gone ahead? Ended their life. I know that I'd be distraught. I'd blame myself. I certainly wouldn't want to share the knowledge with a total stranger."

"It sounds like you *are* trying to put me off."

"No. Graham told me that I wouldn't be able to do that. He said that you were 'a man on a mission'."

"He said that?"

"'A *haunted* man on a mission' if you want me to be exact. I'll be frank with you. I wouldn't normally take on a case like this. Why? Partly because there can't be a happy ending. We can't undo the past and bring Kate back. Also, I can't help but think that bereavement counselling would be a better avenue. There may not even be a 'why?' However, if you are determined to go ahead and – for want of a better word – investigate, then I will help. But I want you to be aware of the pitfalls. You will undoubtedly upset friends and family. It may take months. It may be inconclusive. And if we do reach a conclusion, what if the truth turns out to be worse than not knowing?" Jennings couldn't believe that was possible. Without knowing, he couldn't begin to grieve. Couldn't make sense of this new world he had suddenly found himself in.

****

Jennings arrived at the station early. Wandering into the forecourt's WH Smith, *The Argus* headline was about promotion-seeking Albion's match the following day. A week ago it had been about his daughter. Old news. For some. He popped into the Marks & Spencer to buy Peter's favourite – crispy aromatic duck with a hoisin dip. They'd eaten it on the final night of his visit to Singapore last year. With a dissertation deadline to meet, Kate had decided not to come on the Far East trip. He added a couple of bottles of Sancerre.

Despite the fact that it was mid-afternoon, the station was busy, each train bringing a new flow of arrivals. Relatively few passengers seemed to be departing. There was a mix of commuters, who had sensibly cut short their Friday office grind, and weekenders, seeking out some February fun. That was the thing about Brighton, it had always been a magnet. There were so many sides or faces to it: home to political conferences but also the Festival, Fringe and Pride. There was a darker edge to it as well. The sleepy gentility of Hove just around the corner from seaside riots between Mods and Rockers in the sixties. It had even been there back in the thirties, reflected so menacingly by Graham Greene's sociopath, Pinkie Brown, a character who had deeply disturbed Jennings when he first read *Brighton Rock* as an impressionable undergraduate. Quirky, diverse and sometimes dangerous, the city had always fascinated him. He'd often imagined retiring here. He liked the diversity of the people. He also loved the strange architectural mix: from the madness of Prince Regent's Indo-Saracenic Royal Pavilion, to the Palace Pier, the Clocktower, the fine Regency squares and Victorian seafront hotels.

Kate shared her father's love of architecture, but had always preferred the natural landscape. That was where she had *chosen* to die – he felt that now – and where she had been laid to rest.

There was a tap on Jennings's back. Peter had arrived while he was sat there in a daydream. They hugged, cried and hugged again. The son peered into his father's plastic bag, nodding with approval.

"Good job I didn't become a vegan teetotaller, isn't it?" Only Peter could have found the appropriate style and tone to make a joke about his dead sister, lifting their spirits a little yet maintaining her memory.

****

Plates washed up, a bottle and a half of the Sancerre downed, Jennings and his son had opted to sit on the floor rather than the uncomfortable sofa, which he hoped would serve a better job as Peter's bed for the weekend. He had decided to be totally honest with his son about his thoughts and plans. Peter was the one person he could rely on. His only close family now, as if he needed reminding. He updated him, on the conversations he had had with Graham Miles and Sam Gibb. The wine loosening his tongue, he even suggested that Anne and Marcus seemed ready to move on.

"That's not fair, Dad. And you know it." Jennings opened his arms out by way of apology. "You've no idea what Mum is feeling. Or Marcus. You left us, remember? I was nine, Kate ten. We worshipped you, for fuck's sake. And then you were gone. Like a puff of smoke." Peter sobbed, almost silently, and for the second time in a few days Jennings wished he could take words back which had wounded his son. Arm round his shoulder, he kissed the back of his boy's head. Soothing him.

"I couldn't carry on living in London. A cramped flat in Dalston? Seeing you two every other weekend? You guys didn't want to stay in a crappy bedsit once your mum moved in to leafy, trendy Hampstead with Marcus."

"We didn't care about the accommodation. We just wanted to spend time with you. You must have realised that."

"I know. I felt like a failure. I was angry...and embarrassed. A career going nowhere, a broken marriage, and I couldn't even offer you two a decent second home."

"Selfish. Egotistical."

"Your words, or Mum's?"

"Hers at the time. Mine now. I was young enough to cope okay, to bounce back, but Kate? Girls are more mature, they dig deeper. You know that she started self-harming?" Jennings stared wide-eyed at his son.

"Why didn't anyone tell me?"

"You weren't there. She had counselling. Marcus was a good –"

"Dad?"

"If you want to call it that, yes."

"Why did no one bring the self-harming up at the inquest?"

"She'd stopped. Years ago. She'd moved on. Just like you did. Look, I'm not angry with you, Dad. I sort of understand why you went to Singapore. A new adventure, a professorship, fantastic lifestyle. Far away from Mum. We both loved visiting. But it was never the same as before, was it?"

"No...Your sister didn't come out last year though."

"I've thought about that. Not at the time. But since...she died. There's something I want to show you."

Peter placed his tablet on the floor in front of them. He went on to his *Facebook* account, then transferred onto Kate's. Jennings had briefly joined *Facebook* a few years before, mainly to be able to see any photos or news posted by his children. However, once he had accepted friend requests from a bewildering number of old school acquaintances, work colleagues and former students, the general banality of the users had driven him away. It was the mixture of mundane postings – 'I went shopping an hour ago' – one-upmanship photos from exotic locations or expensive restaurants, and the modern malaise of dirty washing exposed in public. It had both depressed and disturbed him. He had never tried *Skype*, didn't like the idea of looking at someone while speaking to them remotely. Nor did he like the impersonal nature of e-mails. They were fine for exchanging facts and files but not for anything emotive. You couldn't judge someone's mood or tone. Maybe Peter was right: he was a Luddite, or technophobe. Nevertheless, phone calls and good old fashioned letters had enabled him to keep in touch with Peter and Kate on a regular basis over the past few years.

Kate's cover photo and profile picture were the same image of an Antony Gormley sculpture, *Another Place*. Another link. Another memory. The three of them had visited Crosby Beach a few years back. It had been a wonderful day. They sat there watching the hundred iron men facing out to sea, the figures slowly submerged as the tide came in. They had all agreed that this was far from dead art. Cast from Gormley's own body, you had the real sense that they were constantly changing. The weather, time of day and the quality of light altered the spectacle. The sculptures had even aged, their colour changing and barnacles growing on them. It had been a crisp winter's day and they'd had the beach to themselves. After sunset the night-time orange glow from Liverpool Docks had made the experience even more magical.

Peter pointed out his mother's announcement, posted the day after he had been alerted about Kate's death by gossip on *Twitter*:

'It breaks my heart to inform everyone that my darling daughter Kate has passed away. She was and will always be loved dearly. Please feel free to express your own grief or share happy memories here on Kate's account.'

Beneath, a number of people had added brief comments – such as 'so sorry to hear this' or simply 'RIP'. Many had even 'liked' Anne's comment. Jesus Christ! He scrolled back to Anne's words: 'passed away'. That time-honoured euphemism. Had it been used to maintain privacy, in the all-too public world of social media? To avoid offending or shocking anybody? Or from a sense of cowardice? Embarrassment? What would he have done in his ex-wife's place? Precisely the same thing. Suicide – just as it had been in ancient times – was a word that dared not speak its name. A taboo. In Classical Athens you were buried alone, anonymously, on the edge of the city. Marginalised even in death. In Rome you were deemed an enemy of the state. Had things changed that much?

What Peter really wanted to show his father was further back. He explained that he hardly ever used *Facebook*. He preferred to text Kate. However, since her death he had searched through her history on the site. For years, Kate had used it on a daily basis, sharing quotes from authors, photos from historical sites, updates on personal projects, even the odd selfie. She also belonged to a number of 'closed groups' dedicated to specific topics: canals, Victorian society, various novelists, even Laurel and Hardy. However, she had barely posted or shared anything in the last year. There was a photo of her with a round-faced, auburn haired, middle-aged woman – posted in July as 'friends' – but with no name tagged. Peter didn't recognise her. Back a further month there was another picture, of an arty looking couple posing in Breton sailor tops and wearing berets – again unnamed. That was the sum total. In ten months. In this bizarre, virtual world she had gone from animated contributor to silent – absent? – almost overnight. April 2016. Had she simply become bored with the virtual world? It seemed unlikely. Unlike Jennings's generation, Kate and Peter's had grown up in a computerised reality, where texting, tweeting and trending were an intrinsic part of everyday life. No, it might be irrational, or clutching at proverbial straws, but Jennings felt convinced that something had happened in the real world, something which had changed her outlook on life, sent shock waves which reverberated even into her virtual one. Peter returned them to Kate's cover photo, *Another Place*. He was convinced that she had changed it fairly recently. Despite that memorable day, Jennings knew that there were other Gormley sculptures she preferred – the colossal hilltop landmark *Angel of the North* which they had visited on the same trip, or *Field*, the thousands of tiny clay figures crammed into a whitewashed gallery. Why *Another Place*? Now, more than ever, it seemed a darkly ironic choice.

SEVEN

It had been wonderful to spend the weekend with Peter. Their easy relationship over the three days had sent Jennings time-travelling back to the carefree days out they had enjoyed when the kids were little, a private world of fun, adventure, discovery and unconditional love. In reminding him what sort of a father he had once been, it had, naturally, added a sense of both elegy and guilt. Peter had virtually said it, hadn't he? Having provided them with so much, and received so much in return, his children had lost an irreplaceable source of affection and support when he moved abroad. Was his current quest part of an almost Catholic sense of blame or self-reproach? He tried to dismiss the suggestion, but failed.

The 14:58 train from Brighton to London was barely half full. Jennings had a four person table area to himself, and spent the journey rehearsing the evening which lay ahead. Sam Gibb had warned him that if he went ahead 'turning over stones' he would upset people and he knew she was right. How would Anne react when he told her that he had hired someone to ask questions? That her ex-husband was determined to dig his nails into the grief? Sam had contacted a friend of hers, Vince Harrison, who had once worked on *The Argus*. He was now freelance, working as an investigative journalist. Jennings was meeting up with him in an hour's time. Marcus, who had told him that he was about to present himself for selection as a potential Tory M.P., would hardly welcome the prying eyes of the press. Jennings mapped out the next 48 hours in his mind: meeting Vince, dinner at Anne and Marcus', visiting Kate's student flat, and finally a chat with her university tutor. He had agreed to find a few minutes after his afternoon lectures the following day. He had passed the two mystery photos from *Facebook* onto Sam.

Stepping out of the Tube station at Swiss Cottage there was a biting wind blowing, reminding him that it was midwinter in England. Back in Singapore he had become accustomed to the lack of seasons, constant temperatures and the tropical humidity. Initially he had missed the seasonal changes, particularly autumn's mists and the poetic beauty of the landscape. It was hard to beat a Sunday morning walk in the woods, or on the Heath, your breath visible and the crunch of leaves underfoot. As a prelude to winter it carried a cyclical sense of time passing. However, he certainly hadn't missed the freezing cold winter mornings, the frozen windscreens, or the icy roads. He needed to buy a decent overcoat and scarf, items he had simply forgotten about over the last decade.

Adamson Road was a relatively quiet residential street, the large imposing houses, with steps up to equally grand front entrances, had mostly been converted into flats. The Best Western had tried to maintain its former life as a Victorian town house. The bar/lounge reflected the building's origins, furnished with heavy antiques, oil paintings and a grand piano. It was empty, although the receptionist had told him that the hotel itself was full. He had booked in for two nights, although he hoped to only stay for one.

Vince Harrison had sent him an e-mail with a link to an article written by a *Vanity Fair* journalist, Alex Shoumatoff, back in 2009. It explored the suicides of dozens of teens within a ten mile radius of Bridgend. While acknowledging that the misty lowlands of South Wales had always seen a lot of suicides, it asked the reader to examine this current 'malaise' in a different light. Twenty-five 15-28 year olds had taken their own lives, all but one by hanging, a method which apparently young women nearly always avoided. How could this 'cluster suicide' be explained? Rather than a large number of unrelated, individual acts, there seemed to be a definite pattern. The journalist highlighted the fact that outbreaks of a suicide epidemic have occurred throughout history, from Ancient Greece to the first examples of an Internet Suicide Pact in Japan back in 2000. Eight years later a new contagion in Japan had seen a staggering thousand people taking their own lives through inhaling toxic fumes. Apparently Freud had lectured on teenage suicide clusters nearly a century before. Like any decent journalist or writer, Shoumatoff had avoided simplistic conclusions. The presence of a pattern in Bridgend was beyond dispute, but that didn't mean that there had been an almost cult-like pact. Any number of reasons – or combination – might explain each young person's deadly decision: 'life in a backwater', the depressing weather of 'damp mists', divorce, 'empty time', the inability to access the American Dream, a romantic teenage break-up, a (shared?) hope that there existed a better world beyond this one, even genetic changes. Various experts had offered their views on this geographical suicide, including the lack of social mobility in our class structure; an education system which rewarded the already advantaged. The virtual world of social media had played a key role, it seemed, despite youngsters denying that there was an Internet Cult: kids writing eulogies to friends or even strangers and then killing themselves soon after. Was this part of a romanticizing of suicide? Or did it simply reflect a lack of hope for people stuck in a virtual world while the real one couldn't provide what they wanted? One girl commented: "Suicide is just what people do here because there is nothing else to do." Christ! Was it that bad for young people living in the valleys? What sort of a world was Jennings living in where people seemed to be encouraging others to kill themselves, posting 'recipes' for how to die 'easily and beautifully'? Were, as *Time* magazine's international cover story suggested, Britain's youth 'unhappy, unloved, and out of control'? Jennings closed his eyes.

The article had disturbed him. Stuck in his ivory tower in Singapore, he hadn't even realised that these suicide clusters had occurred, either in South Wales or Japan. Nevertheless, apart from the fact that Kate had killed herself, he couldn't see any connection between her death and The Bridgend hangings. His daughter hadn't been living in the damp lowlands of a rural community; she had been in the heart of one of the world's most vibrant cities. Rather than being socially disadvantaged, she had enjoyed a private education and was ambitiously planning for a life as a university lecturer. She was an atheist, which probably ruled out any belief in moving on to some sort of utopian paradise; there was no history of depression, never mind suicide in their family. Yes, Anne and he were divorced, but that had been a decade ago. They had all moved on. Hadn't Peter said that?

Jennings suddenly thought back to Peter's revelation about Kate self-harming. He had inferred that this was a result of their dad moving away. Yet he had assured his father that she had received help and had stopped this. Jennings had looked at some websites which examined self-harm that morning. The search had simply left him more confused. Some experts suggested that self-harming had no connection to suicide; that it was usually to relieve unbearable tension, express distress, or administer self-punishment. Sometimes it was even a cry for help. However, he had also read that over half the people who kill themselves have a history of self-harm. So what had Kate's self-harm represented? Had it been connected to the family break-up? Or Jennings leaving the UK? Was it what they called a 'suicide gesture' in which the aim was not to die? Or had it been a warning, or fore-echo?

A pencil-thin, tall man with spiky white hair and dressed in a long black leather coat entered the room. He nodded a greeting and approached.

"Dr. Jennings, I presume?" Having risen to greet him, Jennings smiled and pointed to the armchair next to him. Vince Harrison sat down, placing a laptop on the coffee table. He smelt of soap and positively radiated energy, almost crackled with it. Jennings felt as if you could have fed off it. "Did you read the *Vanity Fair* article? Wondering why I asked you to read it?" Jennings admitted that he had failed to find any close links or common ground, apart from the most obvious one. "It's a haunting piece, isn't it? I was working on the subject of suicide clusters at the time. Would love to have written anything half as good, but Alex got there first. I wanted you to understand that what Shoumatoff produced was what I consider to be proper, investigative journalism. No lurid headlines, no sensationalism, no moral judgement. Asking objective, difficult questions, painting the full picture, challenging the reader. That's what *I* strive for. I've had a brief search online and there doesn't appear to be any current cluster which your daughter could connect to. Obviously that doesn't mean that you should discount her having used sites to share her thoughts or to ask for help."

"You mean these sick bastards who help you on your way, offering handy tips?"

"There are those, of course. It's virtually impossible to close down all the sites and some people firmly believe that they provide a service."

"Do *you*?" Jennings was trying to control a rising sense of anger.

"I don't know. I imagine that they are made up of a wide range of people. Some ghouls, some who are genuinely trying to make it easier for others at the ultimate point of crisis, some hoping to dissuade people from taking that fatal, final step. And others who are, yes, 'sick bastards'. But no, when I said that your daughter might have gone online for help I was thinking of a friend she could trust or an organisation such as The Samaritans."

"I think if she had sought help it would have been face-to-face."

"If she was feeling ashamed, or embarrassed, which is not uncommon, it would be far easier to discuss everything from the anonymity of a keyboard. It would be useful to access her e-mails, search her recent internet history. Have you considered that?"

"Yes. I was planning on looking at her laptop when I go round to her student flat tomorrow."

"Do you know her password? How to trace her history? Know how to uncover any deleted files?" Harrison's rapid fire questions were met by equally swift shakings of the head from Jennings. "I can probably help with that. The password will be the main problem. If we're lucky, once we power her laptop up, we'll be able to simply click on. Most people don't seem to bother with security measures. Apart from investigative journalists!"

"What do you want in return? Sorry, that sounds cynical. I didn't mean it to be." Harrison waved away the apology.

"Beware of Greeks, eh? There may not be a story. It may have just been an action your daughter took, impulsively or rationally. If we do uncover a story, though, I'd be interested in exploring it."

"You know that Kate's stepfather is Marcus Johnson?"

"Head of Imfrax Corporation and prospective MP? Yes, I knew. But I'm not interested in Johnson. It's suicide which interests me."

"Why?"

"Didn't Sam explain? Shit! I would have thought she would have mentioned it. Our only child, my son, killed himself eight years ago, during his Gap Year in Australia."

"I'm so sorry...Sam didn't tell me that. Did you find out what made him do it?"

"No. He hung himself in a pub bedroom in a small Outback town. No note. No financial worries. No obvious mental disorders. He was brainy, handsome – I would say that of course. A place at Oriel, Oxford waiting for him. Two parents who loved him dearly. A pretty, intelligent girlfriend back home. The worst part about it is that the day we found out, I lost the two people I cared about most. My wife simply shut down. Cut herself off from family, friends, me. An 'emotional coma' is what some people call it. George didn't just kill himself that day. He killed two and a half people."

****

It was a ten minute walk up the hill from the hotel into Hampstead's urban village. Jennings had always been attracted to it. It had a cosmopolitan feel to it, with its eclectic mix of restaurants, antique and book shops, and a pavement café culture. It was the sort of place where you might bump into a film actor, artist, composer, politician, philosopher or pop star. As an undergraduate, Jennings had lived for two years in a seedy flat off the Finchley Road, cheap enough for a student, but close enough to Hampstead to enable him to wander through the village and take walks across London's largest ancient parkland, the Heath. He loved the place's rich literary tradition. Lord Byron, Coleridge, Keats, Shelley, Stevenson, Dickens, Wells, TS Eliot, DH Lawrence, Orwell and Huxley had all lived here. One drunken night, after a lively evening in the area's hostelries, he had dreamed that time had collapsed, allowing these incredible writers to come together. He barely remembered the dream now, naturally, but he did recall that Charles Dickens had waxed lyrical about *Nineteen Eighty-Four*. Despite its social exclusivity, Hampstead had a reputation as being the ideal breeding ground for any budding, educated liberal humanist, something which David Jennings had once aspired to be. In those alcohol-fuelled dreams, anyway.

Hampstead had the deepest station on the London Underground and was home to people with equally deep pockets, such as Marcus Johnson. Passing an expensive-looking boutique, Jennings wondered about the village's reputation. Did it still hold true? Or was it yet another of those self-perpetuating urban myths? After all, he was a stone's throw from Bishop's Avenue, home to celebrities, monarchs, and international business tycoons, rather than liberal humanists. As Marcus and Anne were only too well aware, Hampstead was a safe Conservative ward.

While it wasn't the season for the café culture brigade, the high street was busy with both traffic and pedestrians. Jennings was relieved to turn down the pedestrianised Flask Walk which took him towards the yellow stock brick London townhouse where his exwife lived with Marcus. It had been inherited from his father, twenty years before, but Johnson had built up his multi-million corporate hospitality business from scratch, so it would be churlish to begrudge him the lifestyle he had subsequently enjoyed. Not that Jennings hadn't tried. Besides, this had been Kate and Peter's home – a happy, safe home – for half their lives and Jennings knew that he should be grateful towards someone who had willingly taken in another man's children and brought them up as his own. Would he have done the same thing, placed in Johnson's shoes? He doubted it. Then again, he had fallen out of love with Anne, while Marcus had been experiencing the opposite emotion. Maybe his act of kindness had been the ultimate, sacrificial mark of love.

Marcus Johnson answered the door, no tie but a formal shirt tucked into pinstripe suit trousers. The apron he was wearing told Jennings that Anne was probably busy painting in her studio, Johnson pressed into cooking. In fact, Marcus was a great amateur chef and convivial host, enjoying taking on the twin responsibilities. Jennings could easily imagine him as the high-profile local MP, effortlessly welcoming key Hampstead residents to dinner parties where politics and networking would seamlessly go hand in hand.

The bright, open-plan kitchen had a large oak table for intimate dinners and Jennings noted that it was only set for three. It was a relief, given the way he anticipated the evening conversation going. Johnson poured him a generous gin and tonic before heading out to the hallway and calling for Anne. She arrived, moments later, in her artist's overalls, pecked both men on the cheek, before disappearing upstairs to change. Was this a strategic move, leaving the two men alone? Jennings had always found it hard to read his ex-wife. The awkward silence which prevailed was almost audible. It reminded him of the polar opposites which had always set them apart. Marcus loved rugby and cricket; he preferred football and tennis. Johnson was a dyed-blue Conservative, Jennings was Labour, at least until Tony Blair began to remind him of Margaret Thatcher. He had written a seminal guide to gay fiction, while the nearest Johnson got to the pink press was the *Financial Times*. In theory, they shared a love of music, but Marcus was an opera lover, Jennings preferring the new romanticism of Visage and Steve Strange.

"Went to Arsenal last week," Marcus offered as an opening gambit.

"Arsenal? I thought you hated football. 'A gentleman's sport played by hooligans' etcetera. You used to call it – "

"Kevball? Yes, I don't like anything about it – the overpaid, cheating Prima Donna players, the loutish fans – but you have to move with the times. A lot of my Asian clients want to take in a match."

"The prawn sandwich brigade?"

"Well, corporate hospitality has moved on a bit from that. Peking duck, sautéed chicken with chilli pepper…"

"I'm surprised they have time to watch the match." Jennings thought of the rows of empty seats at Wembley and Wimbledon at 'sell-out' events, corporate guests busy dining while ordinary fans were unable to buy tickets.

"David, you have to bear in mind that corporate guests and sponsors bankroll these clubs and events. Anyway, how long are you over here for?" Anne had made her way into the room, in a simple but attractive mustard dress, as if on cue.

"Well, that's something I wanted to discuss with both of you."

"Sounds ominous," Anne offered as she took her glass from her husband.

****

Jennings lay in bed, replaying the evening's dialogue. What had started as a 'delicately convivial' dinner had fast descended into a heated argument. He had asked to take a look at Kate's room, before the food was served. Anne had taken him up there, left him to look through what she called the 'box room'. She was trying to lighten the mood of the moment. It wasn't that the bedroom was small, simply that the Johnsons had been over to Kate's student flat and emptied it. Two boxes contained clothes, another two were weighed down with books, while a final, smaller one had electronic devices in it: laptop, printer, mobile and tablet. The clothes and books were destined for a local charity shop. The bed still had sheets and duvet on it, in addition to their daughter's collection of teddy bears, pandas etc. She'd never been interested in dolls. It felt cold, despite the fact that Jennings could feel the warmth from the central heating, could hear it emanating from the old-fashioned cast-iron radiator. He wanted to feel Kate's presence, some part of her lingering in the room. It simply felt empty. Nothing remained apart from the objects themselves. After a few minutes, Jennings picked up the box containing the laptop and made his way downstairs.

Over dinner, Jennings brought up Kate's self-harming. Anne had barked a response which Marcus cut short, stating that they hadn't ever mentioned it because they didn't want him worrying from the other side of the world. It had been discussed at length with her, professional help sought. Whatever the problem had been, it was resolved. But what had the problem been? Why does a 'normal', seemingly happy teenager scratch her arms to the point where school matrons are on the phone and the girl won't, can't, wear t-shirts anymore? Neither of them had pointed the finger of blame at him, simply suggesting that it wasn't easy for teenage girls nowadays, particularly in a culture which placed so many pressures on them.

Jennings had eventually dropped the subject, but over dessert had moved on to introduce both Sam Gibb and Vince Harrison. It was this which had lit the fuse. Lying there, the bedside lamp casting shadows on the antique wardrobe, he shut his eyes as he recalled Anne standing over him, shrieking in his face. He had reacted, of course, referring to the boxes as if the Johnsons were simply moving on by shipping her belongings out. The moment the words escaped his lips he knew how wrong they were, acutely aware of the razor-sharp hurt he was inflicting. Had he even intended it? He had half-expected Marcus to grab hold of him, or accuse him of stirring up scandal which could wreck his potential political career, but Mr Johnson had remained ominously, strangely silent, allowing his wife's anger and pain to pour out.

Jennings now reflected upon how unfair he had been. Why had he said it? Perhaps he had needed to see a reaction, for Anne to display her grief. Something that they could still share. Something that proved that Kate still mattered, still existed. The boxes didn't mean that Anne was 'moving on', that a ten day period of official mourning had been respected and had now been brought to a close. It simply meant that she was unwilling or unable to play the grieving mother portrayed in Hollywood movies, the one who wants to establish an eternal shrine in her dead child's bedroom. Jennings hadn't been able or willing to respect that this was her way of coping. Who was to say that she was wrong and that he was right? Given what had happened in their respective lives over the last ten years, who was he to act as moral judge and jury? Wasn't Anne's way better than Mrs Harrison's, locking herself away in an emotional coma?

The small cardboard box sat on the round, low table in the corner of the room. He had picked it up when walking – almost running – out through the Johnson's tiled front hallway, leaving Marcus to calm down his hysterical wife. That was an image which David Jennings could not blink away.

EIGHT

Vince Harrison sat at the hotel bedroom table, having already charged Kate's laptop at the wall socket. He looked like a man who existed – thrived even – on four hours' sleep, coffee granules, hand-rolled cigarettes and that vibrant energy which had struck David Jennings at their first meeting. Within seconds of firing it up, Harrison was grinning.

"Bingo! Straight in, no password needed." Jennings felt excited, nervous, but also helpless, a hopeless amateur waiting for the professional to deliver his verdict. "My gut instinct is that Kate will have also been permanently logged onto her e-mails. Unless she's accessed them remotely since her last session, then we should be fine." Harrison noted Jennings's blank expression. "Put it down to years of looking into people's hidden histories; mostly dead people, sadly."

"*Eight* years?"

"Yes. George's death didn't just radically change my wife's life. I resigned from *The Argus*, decided to dedicate – no, that sounds almost saintly – *spend* my time investigating stories other people wanted to bury: ethnic cleansing, the treatment of illegal immigrants, cyberbullying, suicide clusters. Shit! Kate has deleted all of her e-mails. Hard deleted them."

"They can't be recovered then, can they?"

"Difficult to tell, but never say no. In general terms, we don't really know how 'trash' is handled. We're talking about stuff which is hidden behind the provider's interface. It varies from service to service. They're not even obliged to tell us. Much like a disk, when a message is deleted it may not actually be overwritten until the space it's using is needed. Theoretically, deleted mail may exist in one form or another within the database for some time. We could make a legal request to retrieve Kate's e-mails from her online service provider. Sam could probably arrange that. You also need to bear in mind that an e-mail, by definition, starts off with two copies: the copy in the sender's Sent Mail folder and the copy that the recipient receives. Deleted e-mails can come home to haunt people... Sorry, that was a stupid word to use."

"Please don't apologise. I wouldn't have known where to start."

"Well, it will certainly take a while. In the meantime, let's have a look at her documents. Mmm, almost nothing at all. I wonder...Bingo again! Thank goodness for recycle bins. Your daughter wasn't as careful with her files. There's a few items in here. Take a pew and I'll restore them." Jennings pulled up a seat and Harrison placed the laptop between them, like a kind pupil at school sharing his book with a newcomer. There were multiple photos in two dated folders: one covered her history project at Devil's Dyke; the other was titled 'Singapore 2015'. Jennings asked to start in 2016-03. There was a single snapshot of Kate outside her faculty Thames-side building. There were no folders for April or May, while in June's there were a couple of photos of the 'arty couple'. One was the image which Kate had posted on *Facebook*. The other was taken against the backdrop of what looked like an artist's studio. In July there was a picture of Kate with the middle-aged, auburn-haired lady Peter hadn't recognised. They were standing in a small car park, outside a single-storey building. Library? Student Union? Clinic? It was impossible to tell. August had a photo which was taken outside a far more impressive modern edifice. The name of it was clear enough, the Museo del Oro. There was a dark haired, tanned girl standing next to Kate. Both were looking at the camera but neither was smiling. A holiday in Spain? Jennings could not recall Kate or Peter mentioning a trip abroad. He thought she had been working all summer at a pub on Highgate Hill.

"That's not Spain," Harrison announced. "It's the Gold Museum. In Bogotá."

"Colombia?" Jennings was shocked. "I'm sure I would have heard if Kate had travelled to South America."

"David. You've got to – for want of a better term – reboot. You need to start thinking of Kate as a stranger. The young woman you *didn't* know. I had to face the same thing with George, and he lived with us for goodness sake. Once they start school, stop seeing home as their entire universe, how well do we really know our own children? Who bullies them at school? How happy are they? Later on, who do they socialise with? Who do they communicate with online, behind closed doors? What goes on in their private worlds, or in their heads? Do they take drugs? Are they in a relationship? Do they tell us everything? Or do they merely grunt the standard responses they think are expected of them? The ones which won't lead to further questions." Jennings nodded. He knew that Harrison was right. Had felt the same for years. "I was there, in Bogotá, a couple of years ago, researching a piece on the connections between drugs, assassinations and street kids. One afternoon, I went into the museum. It's a magical time-capsule. Almost a holy grail. It celebrates the cultures which existed pre-Spanish empire, pre-Colombia. It's a place where history and myth merge. *El Dorado*."

"The lost city of gold?" Harrison answered his question with a shrug.

"A man? A city? A kingdom? An empire? A myth? Who knows? There is an incredible piece exhibited in there – the Muisca Raft. Believe it or not, it was found in a cave by some farmers, back in the sixties. For some, it's a sacred artefact, almost primeval. It's come to represent everything which was violated or crushed by colonial brute force. Some people call it the *El Dorado* Raft." Jennings's head was spinning. He couldn't get a handle on anything. He felt overwhelmed by both the stream of new information and the mysterious photos. From one respect, these were precious, frozen moments of his dead daughter when she was very much alive. However, the other faces and the places were alien to him. They felt like fragments, random pieces from a surreal jigsaw puzzle which he was unable to put together to form a picture, a complete text. Something with *meaning*. As a small child he had sat there on Sunday afternoons, watching his father patiently, painstakingly put together thousand piece jigsaws of coastal town seascapes. He remembered feeling lost, helpless, staring at each one, unable to work out which represented bits of sea, which were sky. The problem was that they all looked the same. His father had passed away a couple of years ago, hadn't even recalled the childhood puzzle-solving when Jennings brought it up at the retirement home on one of his final visits, desperate to claw back a shared memory. It had been as if someone had erased his dad's memory banks. His mind had already closed down, simply waiting for the body to join it. Jennings shut his eyes. He could almost smell the boiled cabbage, could see the glazed eyes staring at a daytime TV show. Rest homes, care homes...whatever name you gave them, it didn't alter the fact that they represented death's waiting room. The hours spent there in the over-heated building had saddened him. In many respects he had sensed that he had already lost his father.

Now Kate was gone too, and her most recent photos weren't even shared memories. They meant nothing to him. He wanted to give up. Almost. Thankfully, the seemingly indefatigable Harrison was more upbeat, as if he was trying to recharge Jennings's failing battery. Devil's Dyke, Singapore, the arty couple, the mystery women, El Dorado. There were, Vince Harrison felt, connections to be drawn out. Jennings was less convinced, but desperately wanted to be sucked in. Was there a hidden, cryptic message, or were they simply photographic postcards sent by a virtual stranger? Sent! Who was he kidding? In most cases they were images which had been buried in her Recycling Bin. Jennings left Harrison to look through the other files and search for discarded e-mails. He was heading off to Kate's student flat.

****

The terraced house was on the 'wrong' side of the Archway Road. Estate agents talked up the London property scene, marketed 'up and coming areas', but who were they kidding? Like any capital city, it had boundaries, borders and frontiers. Cross a busy main road and you could move instantly from a genteel oasis into an altogether different city.

Jennings made his way on foot across the Heath, a middle-aged man stepping into his student past, once again. Past Jack Straw's Castle – he was shocked to see that the enormous, atmospheric pub had now been converted into upmarket £700,000 apartments – along Bishop's Avenue, past Kenwood House, and into Highgate Village. One of his heroes, American actor Richard Bradford, had lived here while filming *Man in a Suitcase*. What had the larger-than-life Texan made of this trendy enclave of North London? No doubt his dawn to dusk shooting schedule had left little time to uncover Highgate's treasures, such as the magnificent Waterlow Park, which he was passing now. Jennings had fond memories of seemingly endless sunny afternoons there, taking Kate and Peter for walks when they were toddlers. The swings, feeding the birds, an ice-cream…simpler times. He even recalled Sir Sidney Waterlow's gift to the public as being 'a garden for the gardenless'. Heading down Highgate Hill he passed Highgate Cemetery, a mini-Montparnasse, its architecture as impressive as its list of residents, which included Karl Marx and George Eliot. Richard Bradford was also dead, having passed away a few months back. Jennings had been planning to meet up with him, interview him about his time in London. He had delayed contacting the actor and now it was too late. He taught students about the concept of *Carpe Diem*, yet when was the last time he had 'seized the day'?

Jennings passed the hospital where his two children had been born – the Whittington – and arrived in Archway. Harrison had described *El Dorado* as history meeting myth. Wasn't this another of those places? It was at Archway where the fictionalised Dick Whittington had heard the Bow Bells ringing and turned back to London, while the hospital had been named after the real-life Whittington, Richard, Lord Mayor of London, Sheriff. Whittington was a remarkable man who had paid for sanitation in poor parts of the medieval city and financed a hospital ward for unmarried mothers.

Jennings knew that Kate had not been pregnant, but something equally traumatic must have occurred. Dick Whittington had been running away from a life which he found disenchanting. He reached the foot of Highgate Hill, but changed his mind when he heard the bells. Characters ran away in story books, people ran away in real life. As a teenager, Jennings had run away from the all-boys boarding school his parents had sent him to. He'd never regretted his dramatic decision and he'd been able to move on: to a London day school, university and a career he enjoyed. However, despite what he had read over the past few days, he couldn't find any other way of viewing suicide – it was the ultimate, 'no turning back' form of escape. Sitting on that hillside at Devil's Dyke, Kate had chosen to run away in the cruellest possible form. Jennings could not accept that she had simply rejected what life had to offer. It was not in her nature, whatever Vince Harrison and Graham Miles might say about the need to view her as a stranger. He instinctively sensed that she had been escaping from something in the present – rather than rejecting the future. The pull factors of a loving family and her future prospects had not rung loud enough to make her change her decision. In which case, what, or who, had pushed her?

Kate's flat formed half of what looked like a well-maintained Edwardian house. Compared to his own seedy, student accommodation, this was the Ritz. Anne had warned him that there was no landline at the flat, the students each relying on their mobile phone. Jennings had knocked twice, but the sound echoed down the hall. The house felt empty. As he turned away, Jennings was confronted by a short, stocky man in gardening overalls who asked him what he wanted. It turned out that he was Andrew White, Kate's landlord. His initial, hostile suspicion made way for apologetic sympathy when Jennings introduced himself. White took out a set of keys and ushered him inside.

"I don't know what to say, really I don't. The wife and I, we never had kids; collected houses instead."

"How many have you got?"

"Twelve in all. That's twenty-four flats. That's ninety-six rent cheques a month. I can't grumble, although it's a full-time job: gardening, outside maintenance, leaking taps, blocked toilets." Jennings commented on how smart it seemed for student accommodation. "Times have changed. When we started, twenty odd years ago, you changed the carpets every few years and that was about it. Basic lodgings. Cheap and cheerless." White offered a smile. Jennings sensed that this was as close to a joke as the landlord came. "Now they all expect washing-machine, chest freezer, shower *and* bath. One lot last year asked for a bloody dishwasher."

"Did you know Kate?"

"Not really. I only met her twice. Once when she looked round and then again when she moved in, with the other three."

"Three?"

"Yep. All our flats are virtually identical: four bedrooms, shower room, bath, lounge and kitchenette."

"I was sure that Kate only had two flat mates."

"She did. The fourth girl left. Last Easter. No notice. Just disappeared one day. Rather than get someone else in, they agreed to split the rent three ways. Made no difference to me."

"This girl. Could you describe her?"

"Foreign...South American, I think. Medium height. Skinny." Jennings took out his phone and texted Harrison. He asked him to send the photo taken outside the Gold Museum. In the meantime, he wanted to see Kate's old room.

It was bare, apart from a queen size bed, wardrobe, set of three drawers and a desk. As he had done at Flask Walk, he tried to summon up – what exactly? Not a ghost. Just a sense of Kate's presence in the room. Once again, there was nothing. He couldn't even imagine her sitting at the corner desk working. It was simply a student bedroom, no different – Mr. White assured him – from the three other ones. The ninety-five others. The chime of a temple bell alerted him to an incoming message. He showed the landlord the photo and the man nodded. That was her.

****

Jennings took the Northern Line Tube down to Embankment, walking the rest of the way to the Strand Campus. Despite a lifetime in academia, he had never been to King's College but knew it had an excellent reputation. Kate had required three 'A' grades to gain a place on her Liberal Arts course. He wasn't due to meet her tutor until mid-afternoon, but wanted to get a feel for the place where she had been studying for the past two and a half years. Lots of top students dismissed London out of hand, preferring the dreaming spires of Oxford, or Cambridge. Neither could offer a fraction of what King's College undergraduates had on their doorstep: the theatres, museums, the National Gallery, the Royal Opera House, the numerous monuments and world famous buildings, not forgetting the river Thames. The college was very close to London's artery. What had one 19th century politician called it? 'Liquid history'. All manner of things had emerged from the mud and gravel of the river's foreshore: a prehistoric forest, Roman artefacts, unidentified skeletons…at low tide it was London's longest archaeological site. That was another common thread: Kate had shared her father's fascination with the Thames.

Would Kate have bothered transferring onto the District or Circle Line for the nearer Tube station at Temple? Jennings doubted it. He knew that she would have enjoyed the riverside walk from Embankment. He decided to cross over and went as far as the Globe. The oak and thatch replica interested him. He admired the vision and determination of Sam Wanamaker who had battled for decades to see a dream become reality. Real life rarely matches fairy tale story book, though, and the American had sadly died before his project had been completed. Jennings seemed to be seeing death everywhere, even here in the midst of a teeming, bustling metropolis.

He needed to stay positive. The Globe project *had* been finished – even if Wanamaker hadn't lived to see it – and Jennings was determined to bring *his* quest to its end. He didn't want to upset Anne and Marcus again, but he knew that he would if it was necessary. What had he managed to accomplish so far? Well, at least he had a name, Carolina González. Sam Gibb had already promised to look into her sudden disappearance. What did he know about her? Until April 2016 she had been a flat mate's of Kate's in London. She had dropped out of university and by August was in Colombia, which he presumed was where she came from. Could he presume that? Probably. Harrison had confirmed that both her first and family names were common ones in Colombia. Why had she left so suddenly? Unlike the other two flat mates, she must have been a close friend. Why else would Kate have travelled all the way to Bogotá? A trip like that would have surely been a memorable one. Why then was there only one photo on file?

Back at the faculty, Professor Hastings poured them coffee from a stainless-steel cafetière. After repeating the condolences he had offered at the inquest, and engaging in a few moments of polite small talk about each other's research projects, Hastings glanced at his watch. It was an easy to read gesture: I'm a busy man; I don't have anything to offer which wasn't said to the coroner; I barely knew your daughter.

"Professor, I was a bit surprised the other day when you said that my daughter was predicted a 'lower second'. Kate was hoping – with a prevailing wind – to achieve a First." Hastings opened a file on his desktop computer.

"She did excel in her first year modules, with some top marks. I wasn't her tutor then. However, her end of year results last time round were…pretty mediocre."

"How would you explain the radical change?" Hastings shrugged.

"Pupils drop out or under-perform for all manner of reasons. Too much socialising. Complicated love life. Financial worries." Jennings shook his head to each of these theories. "Perhaps she chose modules which didn't interest her as much as she had hoped. Maybe she struggled as the topics became more challenging."

"How would you describe her attitude in seminars or tutorials?"

"I always had the impression that she had read the texts, but I would say that during the past year or so she rarely spoke up. She didn't engage with the other students. She seemed – if you want me to select a single word – withdrawn."

"Withdrawn? When did this start to happen?"

"I don't know that I can put a date on it. This isn't like school. We don't provide effort grades each term, or send reports home to parents. You know how the system works, Dr. Jennings. If students maintain their attendance records, well...beyond that, it's up to them, isn't it?"

"I know. I know. But please, I need *something*. Anything which can help me to make sense of what has happened." Hastings's previously fixed expression changed, lightened a little.

"I'm sorry. I can't begin to understand how you must be feeling...Let me print off her scores: essays, extended essays, exams etcetera." Jennings stood up, walked across the room and looked out of the window. What time did rush hour start these days? It was only half past three but there was already a steady stream of pedestrians and gridlocked road traffic. He thought of Auden's moving *Funeral Blues* poem. When someone we dearly love dies, we expect our mourning to touch everyone around us, like a halo or a wave perhaps. It doesn't, of course. Clocks do not stop, telephones continue to ring, and intrusive sounds are not muffled or silenced. And no one wears black cotton gloves. Outside our little, hermitically-sealed circle, the world has not changed, even if we feel that 'nothing now can ever come to any good.' Richard Hastings cleared his throat, almost apologetically.

"Up until the Easter vacation last year I would say that Kate was on course for a top degree. After that, her results were 'weak'. I do recall her last essay. She picked out plenty of interesting quotations, and offered a very personal analysis of the text. However, she didn't place the text in its social context or cite any existing criticism. It was more like a dialogue between her and the writer. She must have known that it would receive a low mark."

"What was the essay about?"

"Virginia Woolf's *Room Of One's Own*." Hastings printed out Kate's essay for her father.

****

Back in his hotel room, Jennings noted that the laptop was no longer on the coffee table. It was charging at the wall socket for the second time that day. Vince Harrison emerged from the bathroom. His lived-in face seemed to lack its usual vitality. As he moved towards Jennings, he held out a piece of A4 paper, folded in half. Harrison then held his hand up, as if to discourage him from taking it.

"I found this. It was the only Word document left on the system. David, I think you need to prepare yourself. It seems to be a suicide note." Jennings unfolded the paper and read it silently:

'If I commit suicide, it will not be to destroy myself but to put myself back together again.'

He felt a thumping silence in the room. He somehow knew that this had been intended for him to read. At the same time, the words were vaguely familiar. They weren't Kate's. He'd read them before, but in another tongue. It must have been French, because that was the only other language he could speak.

"Is the laptop up to searching a quote?" Harrison nodded. It took seconds to find the source. Antonin Artaud, a French playwright. "I thought I recognised it. The irony is, he didn't kill himself. Well, he may have done, but he was dying of cancer at the time anyway. He had this experimental – some might say crazy – idea for a new style of theatre. No, 'style' is the wrong word. A whole new method and experience. The audience would sit in the centre of a bare room. No stage, props, etcetera. The actors would perform around them, almost pouncing on them. Assaulting their senses with extraordinary sounds and piercing lights. He wanted to strip language, words, of their meaning. His theatre was to be all about sounds, cries and screams."

"Sounds like Theatre of the Absurd."

"Even worse, Vince. He called it Theatre of Cruelty. I'm not even sure if he completed any plays. Let's have a look...Here it is, one radio play, which wasn't even publically transmitted. This is what he said about language: 'All true language is incomprehensible. Like the chatter of a beggar's teeth.'"

"Jesus!"

"He wanted the audience to feel that they were being engulfed, physically and mentally, trapped and powerless in a vortex."

"Do you think that is what Kate was feeling, then? Trapped, powerless, physically and mentally... *engulfed*?"

"Yes. I do. God knows I'd like to think otherwise. But what else can I believe? It sounds like she was in a living hell, and this was her only way – "

"Out?"

"No. It's as she said, suicide was the only way to put herself back together... Shit! I can't think straight. I had this idea, this grand notion that I needed to go out searching for clues. But I was wrong. I'm sure it's all here. Everything you recovered from her laptop. Kate left me all the pieces. I just can't see clearly."

"George was like that after his manic exam revision sessions. He'd sit there for hours until he was almost cross-eyed. Nothing was going in. I used to tell him to move away. 'Take a breather. An hour in front of the TV. Come back when your brain's had a chance to recharge.' Talking of which –". Harrison picked up the laptop and plugged it back into the wall. "Computers and human brains aren't that different, you know. They both need a break, a chance to refresh themselves. The main difference is that laptops don't do a curry and three pints of lager." Jennings smiled, suddenly realised that he hadn't eaten since breakfast. He happily followed Vince Harrison out of the room and onto another of his old haunts, the clogged-up artery otherwise known as the Finchley Road.

****

The curry house was midweek quiet. They had asked for a table well away from the music speakers and were given a pair of cushioned banquettes opposite each other at the back of the restaurant. There was a comfortable silence between the two men as each added a generous dollop of chutney to his poppadum and greedily surveyed the laminated menu.

"I'm going to offer you a couple of pieces of advice. Then we're going to change the subject. Enjoy an evening off duty. Agreed?" Jennings readily nodded. "Tomorrow, when you get back to your place in Brighton -"

"Hove, actually." Harrison smiled, offered a theatrical, seated bow.

"Leave your suitcase to unpack itself. Walk along the beach. Breathe in that bracing February sea air. Take a stroll down the Palace Pier. Play on some of those mindless penny arcade games. When you feel that you've unwound, head into town. Buy one of those large backing boards, the sort the police used to use for murder inquiries. Start pinning up all the jigsaw pieces. Try to make sense of the puzzle that Kate's left you. Left *for* you."

"Sounds good. Only two problems." Harrison looked at him quizzically. "I make that *eight* pieces of advice. And you obviously haven't seen the size of my living room." Harrison guffawed. "So what did you do at *The Argus*?"

"I covered Brighton and Hove Albion. For my sins."

"You're joking. I'd have loved to have been a football reporter."

"Well, there is a downside. I grew up as an Albion fan at the Goldstone. Thought it was the centre of the universe. Then you start covering the matches and it's like stepping behind the stage curtain. You break the magic. You realise it's just a job for the players. When they 'up their game' you wonder if it's because they're playing for a new contract. It makes you a wee bit cynical. Also, my timing was terrible. I arrived as the old board of directors sold the ground. With no new one to move to! You couldn't put it in a novel; no one would believe it! I ended up travelling to Gillingham for 'home' games, a 140 mile round trip. Then they moved to the Withdean, a former zoo turned athletics stadium. Bloody great big running track between the stands and the pitch. You virtually needed binoculars. I must've been the proverbial albatross. The year I resigned they announced the move to a new state-of-the-art stadium at Falmer. I should have written a book about it: 'Vince Harrison: The Wilderness Years'." Jennings chuckled, before calling the waiter over for two more pints.

NINE

By nine thirty the following morning Jennings was carrying out one of Vince Harrison's eight pieces of advice by walking along the promenade. It couldn't be described as a leisurely stroll, amble or saunter. The wind was horizontal and the few brave souls who had ventured out were staggering around like drunks. It reminded him of Charlie Chaplin's short film *The Cure*, where Chaplin plays an upper-class inebriate supposedly drying out at a health spa. His cache of liquor bottles is accidentally thrown into the health spring and innocently slurped by the previously sedate patients. They start dancing around in a haphazard fashion, much as the Brighton brigade were now doing.

Harrison had painted a picture of a 'bracing' walk along the seafront and it certainly was that. He had no idea where it would measure on the Beaufort Wind Scale; somewhere between a strong breeze and a moderate gale? Chaplin brought back memories of Sunday afternoons in North London in the Jennings household. He'd sit on the sofa, with Kate and Peter snuggled up either side of him, the three of them mesmerised by the antics of Chaplin or – more frequently – Laurel and Hardy. Anne would come into the living room as roars of laughter greeted an out of control piano hurtling down a steep flight of stairs, or Stan and Oliver's car being sawed in half. She simply shook her head, baffled by how anyone could find these crude scenarios funny. She had never understood how Jennings could be just as moved by a piece of slapstick black and white comedy as by a deeply philosophical novel.

Had they ever had enough in common to make a happy marriage? Before Kate was born he would have said 'yes'. They shared plenty of interests and passions: eating out; visiting modern art galleries; exploring Paris and Provence; sitting in the shade with a good book, rather than sunbathing on the beach; walking through London parks; watching a piece of *avant garde* theatre. When Anne first moved in with him, they had enjoyed each other's modest, initial professional successes: a short guide to Woolf's *To The Lighthouse* and an exhibition of landscape paintings based around Hampstead Heath. They didn't live in each other's pockets. Saturday saw Jennings head off to football, Anne pottering around town or visiting a fellow artist. However, Sunday was a shared ritual: two hours across the Heath, a pint in the pub, a late-lunch roast, and dozing off with a section of the *Sunday Times*. Simple pleasures. Kate's arrival had changed everything. Overnight. Most parents could probably identify with that to an extent. It didn't matter how many pre-natal classes you attended; nothing prepared you for a first baby's arrival. The all-consuming responsibility.

Kate had rarely slept through the night for the first eighteen months. Jennings had left it to his wife to take on the night-time responsibilities. His argument was that he had to teach all day, while her painting could be done at any time. At first this had not represented a major problem in their relationship, but as the months went by Anne had started to resent their fixed, designated roles. By the time Kate was eighteen months and Peter had arrived on the scene, Anne's twinned role as night nurse and milk provider was over – for Kate – and her daughter had gravitated towards dad for affection and trips to the park. Instead of understanding Anne's feelings of rejection, Jennings had felt an undeniable – if unvoiced – sense of victory. Each day Kate loved him a little more, and Anne loved him a little less. Gradually, they fell out of love. Jennings began to flirt with some of his undergraduates and Anne met Marcus Johnson at the opening night of her first major exhibition, an event her husband missed. He had been looking after the children, but they both knew that it was simply an excuse, a snub.

He didn't care anymore about Anne or her work. And that evening she found another man who did.

Jennings found himself a few yards from the Palace Pier. There had been other piers in Brighton. The Chain Pier had mainly been a landing stage for packet boats, although it did also offer visitors a few simple attractions. Due to be demolished when the Palace Pier was built at the turn of the 20th century, a storm had conveniently finished it off. The West Pier had once been all about grabbing some of that healthy sea air 'Doctor' Harrison had recommended, but it had soon become a magnet for pleasure seekers: a bandstand, then a grand concert hall, tearooms, funfair. Tastes changed, financial corners were cut and the pier had been closed before Jennings first visited Brighton in the late-1970s. As for the Palace Pier, that too had evolved, reflecting the changing times: concert hall, theatre, amusement arcade and roller coasters. Featured in a host of films and television dramas, it represented an iconic image of the town. Now some people were comparing it unfavourably to the i360 observation tower, self-labelled as a 'vertical pier'. A *fourth* Brighton pier? Jennings couldn't see the connection. He'd read Janet Street-Porter's scathing review of it online. It was a well written piece. People often labelled her as a television 'celebrity', forgetting that she was also a top journalist. He'd found himself agreeing with many of her general points about modern architecture. As for the i360, 'eye-sore or post-modern monument?', that was her question. Jennings wasn't convinced that you always had to take sides. For him it was a space-age needle, looking (benevolently?) down on the city. He liked its multi-coloured glow at night. A controversial piece of modern technological art, if it had people talking about it, wasn't that part of its purpose? The Eiffel Tower hadn't been universally liked when it was erected, yet he couldn't now imagine Paris without it. This new building also dominated its cityscape. Live with it and people would probably learn to love it. He admired its bold design and sheer scale, but as a post-modern landmark, not a pier. Unless, of course, the traditional *Carry On* pier had simply had its day and this was its natural successor. What precisely had Street-Porter said about it in *The Independent*? He sat down on a bench with a windshield, glad to be out of the wind, and googled it:

'Traditional Victorian piers generally included cafés and entertainment, a promenade area and seats, slot machines and places to fish, all for a modest entrance fee. A lift just offers a costly trip to a view and then you return to earth and the souvenir shop.'

Love her or loathe her, she had a way of cutting through the commercial and marketing bullshit. Her description of the traditional seaside pier reminded him how fast the world was changing. Jennings wanted to believe that there was still room for the simple, seaside holiday. Surely the seemingly timeless bucket and spade, crabbing, fish & chips, and bed & breakfast could happily co-exist with a high-tech, virtual world of touchscreens and social media? The wind wasn't letting up. Jennings decided not to brave the wooden boards of the pier. Instead, he headed into town to buy a printer and a large board which he could use to pin Kate's clues to.

****

DEVIL'S DYKE

                                                                SINGAPORE

ART STUDIO (WITH?)

                                                 CLINIC? (WITH?)

                                   ?

THE GOLD MUSEUM (CAROLINA)

                                  A ROOM OF ONE'S OWN

THEATRE OF CRUELTY

                                        ANOTHER PLACE

Kate's jigsaw pieces were placed around the edges of the board. For now he had simply typed up titles. The images needed printing off and placing beneath each one.

In the centre, Jennings had originally placed a **WHY?**, but then decided on a large, bold question mark. Why had he decided to use the punctuation mark instead? Were all the pieces there? Or were some missing? Did that matter? It would certainly help if he could fill in the missing names and the identity of the building in front of which Kate had been photographed with the auburn haired woman. It might not be a clinic, but it wasn't a library or Student Union. Richard Hastings had said that he was sure of that, after Jennings had sent him the image.

****

"Jesus, David!" Graham Miles' solid frame stood in front of the inquiry board. "It's like something out of *The Sweeney*. Whose idea was this? No, don't tell me. Vince Harrison?"

"How did you guess?"

"I've known Vince since he was a junior reporter on *The Argus*. Even arrested him once!" Jennings's eyes widened. "He was interviewing a player after a particularly abject Brighton home match. Accused the guy of 'pussy-footing' his way through the game, if I remember rightly. They ended up brawling. In front of the local TV cameras." Jennings laughed.

"That sounds about right. What happened?"

"It took me most of the evening to persuade the duty officer *and* the player to drop any charges. And he was right, of course: the guy was more ballerina than footballer...I've always liked Vince. His heart's in the right place. He passionately believes in things. And people. He's an ethical, morally-sound journalist, which is almost an oxymoron. Seriously, though, is all this a good idea? It looks like a stage set. This isn't a murder inquiry."

"Maybe it is." Jennings held his hand up, as if to ask for the time to explain. "I've been thinking through this for the past couple of hours. Kate's tutor suggested that she could have had relationship problems, but my ex is sure that Kate wasn't romantically involved with anyone. Plus, her flatmates said at the inquest that she had no visitors and rarely went out."

"Have you asked her GP if she was on the pill?"

"No. But I doubt he'd tell me. Would he?"

"Probably not. Particularly as she was over 18." Miles looked at the board again, taking in each photo, one by one. "A female lover?"

"I don't think sex was a driving force for her. Let's say that I'm right, that she didn't have a partner." Miles nodded for him to continue. "Stress from her studies? I've seen her final essay – she handed in something which she knew would fail. She'd given up! This was her oxygen, her dream. Someone must have shattered that. Not simply changed her. Damaged her beyond repair. I'm sure of it. That's why I changed the **WHY?** to a question mark. Behind the **WHY?** is a **WHO?**"

"A cyber suicide group? Radicalisation?"

"She was an independent thinker, not a sheep. She wasn't interested in politics or religion. Her idea of fanaticism was following the *Twitter* feed of certain writers and film makers. No, I think this was something personal."

"You may be right. Maybe someone *had* messed with her mind. Traumatised her. But that doesn't make it murder."

"Vince sent me an article about suicide clusters in Bridgend."

"I remember those."

"Well, the journalist talked about a 'psychodynamic' explanation for suicide. They call it '180 degree murder'. You want to kill someone else…but you eliminate the person by killing yourself. Have you ever heard of someone doing that?"

"Crikey. You don't like simple questions, do you? I mean, in cases of childhood abuse or incest, the perpetrator *is* pushing their victim towards a cliff edge. Some grow up to commit the same crimes. Others manage – somehow – to move on. But some decide that they can't face the future. Is that murder? Manslaughter? How do you measure it? Is suicide always the result of an external force? Or are some people genetically wired for it?…Bloody hell! I'm beginning to sound like Vince. David, in my line of work I see damage all the time: cars, houses, *and* human beings. You can mend or replace the others, but people…Young suicides are the worst. You always ask yourself the same thing: 'Why?' But at the end of the day, it's not like a car accident, house fire or a terminal disease. Suicide is a choice. Whether you jump off a bridge or walk into a night club with explosives packed around your body. Fear, desperation, a sense of hopelessness, radicalisation?…How many possible reasons are there? Most don't leave a note, as you know. We can't ask them what pushed them, or pulled them. Kids are more impressionable than we are. These youngsters don't have the life experience, the wider world view needed to put problems into some sort of wider context. It never gets any easier, though, I can tell you that. The minute it no longer matters to me, I'll be out. Have you spoken to Sam about this?

"No. Why?"

"I hope I'm not speaking out of turn. She might be willing to shed some personal light on what it's like." DI Graham Miles refused to be drawn any further, instead making the sign of a mobile phone call. "Ask *her*."

****

Sam Gibb sat on Jennings's unforgiving sofa bed, seemingly oblivious to any discomfort. Oblivious to anything, outside of a painful, buried memory from the past which Graham Miles and Jennings had just brought back to the surface, like sadistic archaeologists. Her eyes were red-rimmed. Having listened to her story, Jennings felt emotionally exhausted, drained. He couldn't begin to imagine how she was feeling.

For the past hour she had mentally time-travelled back to a series of events which had taken her to the verge of suicide. So close, in fact, that she said it was only thanks to two 'Angelic Samaritans' that she had found a way to cope, and move on. The story involved both Graham Miles and Vince Harrison. The connective tissue between the four of them seemed to be thickening, beginning to bind them together.

Gibb had still been working as a solicitor at the time. She had been given a client called Craig Tosh, a man who had become one of the very first internet millionaires. A business-savvy, middle-aged wide-boy who liked to 'play away from home', she had taken an instant dislike to him from their very first meeting. He had a habit of looking at women as if they were pieces of meat hanging in a butcher's shop. Married with two young children, he'd got some local gangster's daughter pregnant. "Need a quick divorce and re-marriage in order to avoid a concrete overcoat. Or worse." He had laughed about it, as if it was a minor playground misdemeanour. Sam had asked to be relieved of the case, but the senior partner of the firm had told her in no uncertain terms that it was her responsibility to do what she could for the client, regardless of her personal views. Morality was neither here nor there. She had fulfilled Tosh's request, agreed an 'amiable settlement' with his wife, and the businessman had – seemingly – been pleased with the outcome, ready to move on to his expectant child bride. She recalled the clamminess of his hairy hand, the way it had lingered for a second too long, and the expression of undisguised lust in his pinprick, dead eyes. He had asked her to join him for a 'champagne celebration' lunch. Thankfully she had another client already waiting, making it easy to turn him down. What had been his response? 'Your loss', or something like that.

She had left the office early that afternoon, about half-past three. On one of the stone steps down to her basement flat there had been a bunch of hand-delivered flowers. No name on the card. However, the message – 'BETTER THAN BUBBLY?!' – had given him away. Which was no doubt his intention. How had he discovered her home address? She rang the office, feeling flustered. Both the secretaries and the two other solicitors were adamant that they hadn't passed her personal details on to anyone. She was ex-directory and prided herself on the way she kept her professional and private lives separate. Like Dickens' John Wemmick, she liked to pull up the drawbridge when she reached home, even if hers was only a metaphorical one. She was convinced that he must have followed her home one evening.

Her first instinct had been to throw the dozen red roses into the bin. There was no way she was keeping them in her home, a constant reminder of a creep like Tosh. However, she hated waste and the following morning divided them into identical gifts for the two secretaries – peace offerings to make up for grilling them over the phone. That evening there was an envelope stuck under her front door. The message left little to the imagination: 'THE FLOWERS WERE FOR YOU – YOU UNGRATEFUL BITCH!' Gibb had sat down, feeling nauseous. She was emotionally torn, caught between fury and fear. With hindsight she should have told someone. The senior partner? The police? The problem was that although she knew deep down that Craig Tosh was responsible, she had no proof. Two typed, anonymous messages. Neither of the leaseholders of the flats above her had seen anybody hanging around. Why would they? She never went into the main part of the house, nor did any of her visiting friends. The private steps and entrance had been part of the attraction when Gibb bought the Hove garden flat. Now her cosy home felt like a trap, crackling with potential menace.

A month passed by, uneventfully. Then the daily phone calls had started. Late at night. Not a word said, not even the clichéd heavy breathing. Just a thumping silence which, if anything, felt worse. After a week of almost sleepless nights, there had been an event which she would never forget. It had been a fraught day at the office and she had returned home late, in the lashing rain, only to discover a break-in. No major items had been taken, such as the television or hi-fi. Instead, all of her personal knick-knacks and ornaments had been smashed, ground into the carpets. And Dolby, her cat and companion, lay in a pool of blood. A policeman arrived within minutes. DI Graham Miles. Although back then he'd only been a DC. He'd made her a cup of tea, called a vet and the RSPCA. A fingerprint team had dusted the place. Dolby had been put to sleep and Sam Gibb had told Miles about the previous incidents. He asked her if she felt up to outlining her suspicions all over again, and that was when Vince Harrison had been called in. He'd recently lost his son and resigned from the local paper. Tosh was known to both men from a couple of outbreaks of football hooliganism which he had been suspected of orchestrating. On neither occasion had he been caught on camera and he had a seemingly cast-iron alibi for both times when the actual trouble kicked off.

Miles and Harrison insisted on clearing up the debris while Gibb tried to make a list of all the items which were broken. Worthless objects from a financial point of view, but many of them holding priceless sentimental value. Afterwards, the three of them sat at the round kitchen table. It was Miles who broke the silence.

"Craig Tosh is a sick bastard, if you'll excuse the language. Unfortunately, he's not stupid. He's got the narrow intelligence of a weasel. I'll bet that the only fingerprints we find here will be yours."

"I have an idea," Harrison interjected. "The house opposite. The empty one with scaffolding?" Sam Gibb nodded. It was being converted into flats. "Peters and Son. Family building company. They did some work on our place a few months back. Kitchen extension. I was trying to bring my wife, Mary, back into the here-and-now. Give her a Delia Smith kitchen. She used to love cooking…The builder, Malcolm Peters, is a nice bloke. I think I could set up a little bit of surveillance from the top floor window. We need to catch the sicko on camera."

"What worries me, Sam, is the escalation. Seemingly-jovial note, abusive message, threateningly silent calls, now smashing your lovely home and killing the cat. What next?" Graham Miles hesitated, not wanting to terrify her, but needing to make it clear that he doubted Tosh would stop there. "We need to catch him before anything else happens."

"I don't know what to say. I've never met either of you before and you've being incredibly kind. And you've believed me. But I'm not sure how much more I can take. I'm scared to walk home, terrified at the thought of sleeping here tonight. I feel violated, and as for Dolby – " Gibb was unable to go on. Vince Harrison lightly stroked her back, while he and Miles shared a worried look. Sam Gibb was a young woman on the edge of an emotional precipice. And with good reason.

The following day, Graham Miles organised a patrol car to pass by every hour, while Vince Harrison began to operate from the house opposite, from midday to midnight. He insisted that it would be a relief to have a 'project', refused any payment. As it turned out, however, the worst was yet to come.

Sam Gibb had a patio which was accessed from the glazed double doors of her kitchen. She hadn't used it since receiving the envelope. After the first nocturnal phone call, she hadn't even raised the blinds, thus cutting off the room's only natural source of light and plunging her into the literal dark.

It was two days after the break-in, a gloriously sunny late afternoon in June and Gibb had decided that she wasn't going to be a prisoner in her own home. As she lifted the blinds she was immediately aware of a pair of brown leather cowboy boots. Lifting her gaze, there was Craig Tosh, his right hand inside his trousers, his eyes fixed on her. He winked, a chilling, sexually aggressive gesture. He then turned and left, sauntering away, coldly casual, and presumably hurdling the back garden fence. Gibb ran to the phone, asked for DC Graham Miles, before collapsing on the sofa.

Half an hour later Craig Tosh was arrested. Grinned confidently. No request for a lawyer. Questioned. Another alibi tossed in, this time from the child bride. No concrete evidence. Freed. Miles phoned his apologies through to Sam Gibb. He pictured her on the other end of the line; wondered how close to the edge she was standing.

Eventually Tosh was caught out. In the end it hadn't been a vigilant policeman or Harrison's surveillance. Malcolm Peters's son, Jason, on a 'crafty fag' break, had caught sight of a stocky figure in a hoodie descending the basement steps, went to investigate, and confronted Tosh while the latter was levering open the front door. Tosh served six months, while Jason Peters served eighteen for GBH, despite the handfuls of testimonies to his good character and kind nature. Unable to simply 'move on'. Gibb had sold her home, resigned from the solicitors' office, set up her inquiry agency and moved into the basic attic flat above her new business. Seven and a half years on, her home town still seemed like an alien place, one where lone, male strangers passing her in the street wore the faces of potential stalkers, rapists and perverts.

"I was close, very close to cutting out the source of my pain, my abuser, by killing myself. '180 degree murder' might be the buzz term, David, but for me it would simply have been to end the nagging fear that Tosh, or someone like him, could target me again." Jennings realised that he hadn't opened up Sam Gibb's wound. It had never healed. Maybe it never would. "I hope to God that Kate didn't encounter a Craig Tosh. Had I been twenty at the time...had it not been for Graham and Vince...and Lorna."

"Lorna?"

"Lorna Myers. We met at a Working Women's retreat in Manhattan. We were – briefly – lovers. I suppose that I was on the rebound in a strange way, fuelled by an anti-male blind hate. And I was curious. But I'm not cut out to be gay. Lorna, on the other hand...She spends the summer months taking full advantage of the Brighton LGBT 'scene'."

"And winter?"

"Ah. Winter is spent hibernating under her pen name, Beverly Bronte. Since our fling, we've become best friends, blood sisters and, for the past three years, flat mates. From my office you can usually hear her typing away furiously in the spare bedroom: rapid-fire crime thrillers featuring a female private detective. The protagonist is a lesbian. Gutsy, cerebral, sexy. It's autobiographical! Exquisitely written, but beach novels, nonetheless: easily consumed, instantly forgotten. Not the sort of books you'd want to analyse. 'Mass market murder from the Badwoman in the Attic'. Her words, not mine! She used to be a profiler. She's…unconventional, intimidating, but lovely!"

"She sounds…interesting. But Sam, how is a pulp fiction novelist meant to help me?" Gibb smiled, tapping the right side of her nose.

****

Sam Gibb had headed back to her office. Hopefully her heavy workload would allow her grief to return to its shallow grave. Sadly, Jennings doubted it ever stayed there for long.

Lorna Myers didn't fit the mental image which Jennings had – irrationally and stereotypically – formed. When Gibb had told him about the lady from Houston, he had pictured a stern, short, butch woman, a JR/Miss Marple hybrid. In reality, Myers was about his height, slim, handsome, with prominent cheekbones. Her accent was more educated New York than Texan drawl, as if she had carefully reinvented herself. Her smile revealed American dentistry and she immediately put him at ease.

She was talkative, happy to fill in some of the details of her extraordinary life. Her parents and siblings were all involved in the traditional Houston industries of aeronautics, gas and oil. They were a close-knit, loving family but also active members of a conservative, traditional Bible belt community. Myers had known that 'coming out' would spell the end. She would be kicked out of home, ostracised by the local community. For three years she had tried her best to conform: regular job, boyfriend etcetera. However, that was never going to last. It was a living death. Maybe worse than ceasing to exist.

Having saved enough money to apply to a higher education institution, she left home to uncover a sexual world she had fantasised about for years, and to study Offender Profiling. She found herself fascinated by criminology and psychology, but frustrated by the detached role of the profiler. She was expected to develop the skills of an investigative scientist, interested in the psyche of the criminal. As a police profiler, she would be looking for types, rather than specific criminals. Myers knew that the minute she arrived at a murder scene she would feel the need to burrow into the core of the investigation, be part of the team who narrow the search down to individual suspects, rather than simply theorising about typologies. Besides, too many profilers seemed to make dangerous assumptions and sweeping generalisations based on ethnicity, gender, class, even sexuality. She completed her degree, toed the line in her essays and was awarded a top degree. However, after six months working in New York, she handed in her notice, jaded and frustrated. She met Sam Gibb on a retreat, moved to the UK and started writing. Her fictional heroine, BA Mason – a lesbian profiler/private eye who investigated 'pink crime' in the Big Apple – allowed Myers the freedom to be the detective she wanted to be, without any of the restrictions, bureaucracy or paperwork.

Having already been given the background information on Kate's suicide by Gibb, Myers asked Jennings to take her all around the photos on the outside of his board, filling in the unwritten text.

"This is Devil's Dyke. We went there every few weeks when Kate and Peter were little. The photo is from when she went back there as a student for a history project, on how the social use of landscape alters. She enjoyed piecing the past together, finding connections across the ages."

"So, happy times."

"Well, not entirely. It's where she killed herself."

"That doesn't taint it, David, however bizarre that might sound. It simply means that it was somewhere she felt safe. Almost a chora."

"Like a womb?"

"Possibly. The chora's a safe space, with maternal, protective implications." Jennings nodded and moved on to the second photo.

"That's my apartment block in Singapore." He hesitated.

"And?"

"And – she didn't come out last Easter. First year she'd missed. She had booked this year's trip though."

"It's quite the opposite of a chora. I mean, it's a skyscraper. Phallic. Male. I know, you think I'm over-interpreting it. Freudian psycho-babble. Perhaps. Maybe it simply represents the absent male – you!" Myers moved on to the third picture. "This art studio's interesting. Sam didn't mention Kate being a painter."

"She wasn't. Drawing was something my father and grandfather were good at. And her mother is a successful artist. But Kate, like me, was useless."

"Why was she there, then? And who are the couple?" Jennings shrugged. "We need to find out. Discover the location, and we'll soon unravel their identities."

"Which is more important? The place or the people?"

"Hard to say, but my educated guess would be the place, and how Kate interacted with it. I mean, what she was doing there. Same with this other building. It looks medical, but what does that tell us? Was she after birth control pills? An HIV test? The smear? Why did she need a companion with her? Who is she? A mature student at the university? Her best friend? Lover? We need to get Sam asking questions about these two photos." Moving on to the next picture, Myers nodded. "Vince told me about the Gold Museum." Myers noted Jennings's surprise. "We're both key members of Sam's ever-decreasing circle, as she likes to call it. I think this one links to Devil's Dyke."

"What's the connection?"

"The museum's full of gold artefacts. But they're more than simply objects. Vince said that they represent a precious, happier time, before colonialism arrived. A lost world. Another protective place. Another chora. What about the other student, though? What did she mean to Kate?" They moved on, the question left to hover. Jennings had pinned up a photo of a Woolf front cover to represent Kate's final essay.

"*A Room of One's Own*... Virginia Woolf."

"Jesus, David! I do know who Virginia fucking Woolf is! I'm a militant lesbian and feminist writer for Christ's sake! Woolf's almost my Earth Mother!" Myers' smile told him that the comment was heartfelt but that she was also striving for levity. Teasing him. "When you think of that book, what springs immediately to mind?"

Jennings knew that they were both thinking about the same character, a remarkable figure who Woolf had invented in order to make a powerful, polemical point – Judith, Shakespeare's sister. In Woolf's haunting tale, Judith is as naturally gifted and talented as William. However, while he enjoys a formal education – grammar, logic, Classical literature – and has the freedom to roam and hunt, Judith is stuck at home, mending stockings and minding the stew. Rejecting her father's arranged marriage plan, the sixteen year old runs away to London, hoping to join a theatre. At the stage door she is mocked and ridiculed, denied access. Finally, the actor-manager 'took pity on her' – forces himself on her? Jennings knew the final lines by heart:

'She found herself with child by that gentleman and so – who shall measure the heat and violence of the poet's heart when caught and tangled in a woman's body? – killed herself one winter's night and lies buried at some cross-roads where the omnibuses now stop outside the Elephant and Castle.'

Both Judith and Kate were young women who had killed themselves. But the fictional Judith Shakespeare and the real Kate Jennings had little else in common. Kate had received the same education as her brother, had enjoyed the same freedom. There had been no arranged marriage. No barred door or glass ceiling preventing her from living out her dreams. She even had *two* rooms of her own. Jennings passed his daughter's final essay on to Myers, who took out a pair of reading glasses and sat down, quickly transferring from sofa to floor. She read through it twice, methodically, before placing the A4 sheets on the ground and removing her glasses.

"You can see why her tutor failed her. No references to critics, or contemporary writers, no contextualisation. It's the essay of someone who has given up."

"You really think so? That's bullshit, David! Sorry, but you really haven't read this properly. It's magnificent. It's challenging. It's exciting. She's understood Woolf's argument and communed with it. Who cares what other critics have to say? That's second hand material. Boring! This is an outstanding, highly intelligent, eloquent response to a like-minded spirit. This is what you people should be encouraging: original thought. Not asking students to robotically catalogue and drip-feed what other people have already said. This essay lives, breathes."

"What are you saying? That rejecting the established methodology was a good idea?"

"Rejecting the status quo is often the best possible response – the *only* meaningful response – to our bullshit society, David. How else can things change? We're petrified nowadays to step out of line, in thought, speech or the written word. Free expression is frowned upon. And academia is part of the malaise. Kate was rejecting the crap thrown at her, forced on her, not turning her back on academic life itself."

Myers and Jennings examined the penultimate photo together. Jennings had printed off an image of The Theatre of Cruelty to go with his daughter's (suicide?) note.

"This is the polar opposite of having a room of one's own. Here you're surrounded, hemmed in. Physical and mental entrapment. It's horrible, claustrophobic." Jennings nodded in agreement.

"What about the final one? *Another Place*? We went there a few years ago. On our very own Anthony Gormley tour."

"Well, it's another contrast. Here the art is outside. There's freedom. You can move around at will to view the figures. Identical *male* figures. Is that significant? Then again, perhaps it just brings us back full circle. Like the Dyke, it's a happy memory, one shared by the three of you. They're both panoramic landscapes. The sea is another chora. People say that the sound of waves takes us back, subconsciously, to the womb, don't they?"

"Do you believe that?"

"It doesn't matter what I think. It's what Kate thought that should concern you."

****

Had Lorna Myers' visit been helpful? A problem shared? Or had it simply posed more questions, deepening the puzzle? Everything in the photos seemed to revolve around either wide open places or cramped inside spaces. Jennings made his living from interpreting texts and signs. So why couldn't he read between the lines here? Myers was convinced about two things, though. First, that Kate had set the puzzle up for *him*. Second, that he needed to identify the mystery people and talk to each of them, and the Colombian girl. Until then, the jigsaw would remain incomplete and unintelligible.

Why had Kate set up this elaborate maze? Lorna Myers suggested that it proved his daughter had been sound of mind, lucid, despite whatever inner turmoil had taken her to the point of no return. Yes, he agreed, that was beyond doubt. Yet there was more to it than that. Jennings now saw it as a test, one set by a distraught daughter for her absent father. 'How badly do you want to know, Dad? Is it *really* important for you to find out WHY?'

Later, lying in bed, trying to drift off to the sound of the waves, he realised that it *had* been good to meet Lorna Myers. Talking to someone outside his bubble, a perfect stranger, helped. In a vague, indescribable way. Outside, it was a stormy night and the sea was rough, savage. The sound of the womb? No, it felt as if he was being lashed by tidal waves of suicide. It was everywhere, invasive. Virginia Woolf had drowned herself, filling her pockets with stones. Some of her most memorable fictional characters, like Judith Shakespeare and Septimus Smith, had killed themselves. Sam Gibb and Lorna Myers had contemplated it. Vince Harrison's son had hung himself. Graham Miles investigated self-murders. He'd been there at the Chapel of Rest, Kate's doorkeeper. Jennings needed to close the window, shut the waves out. He needed to sleep.

TEN

Jennings was lying on the beach. Kate and Peter were squealing with laughter as they buried him in the sand. Anne wasn't in sight. Had she gone back to the hotel? Had he upset her? He couldn't remember. He shut his eyes, grinning as the grains sprayed against his eyelids. Suddenly the splattering stopped. The toddlers' little spades had ceased digging. He opened his eyes to two bored teenagers looking down at him. They were asking to go home. This didn't make any sense.

Now he was in the sea. The current was pulling him away from the beach and he was panicking. Peter was a toddler again, screaming out to him. Gormley's iron men were standing around, but in a circle, their faces looming down on Kate. One picked up her lifeless body, placed some seaweed around it like a wreath, while the others began to dig a hole in the sand. A grave. Peter's screams grew louder, as Jennings drifted further away from the shore. He was underwater now, the sea cold and grey. He was sinking. It was futile. He stopped struggling. It almost felt good to let go.

Then he felt himself rising up, through layers of water. No, layers of sleep. His phone was ringing. He took a moment to register the fact that he had been dreaming, before grabbing hold of his mobile and squinting at the screen. It was Sam Gibb.

"Yes?"

"You sound rough."

"So would you if you'd been inside my head a few seconds ago. Stephen King couldn't better the nightmare I was having."

"Then you have *two* reasons to be grateful to me this fine morning." Jennings sat up, dug some sleep out of his eyes. "The arty couple? I have names and an address."

Once again Jennings found himself heading up to London on the train. Gibb had sent the photo as an e-mail attachment to every gallery, art museum and studio in the Greater London area and Metroland which she could find; well, the ones which offered an electronic address.

Dear Sir/Madam,
I appreciate that you are busy and no doubt receive requests for information or help on a daily basis. However, this is a matter of the utmost urgency. I am attempting to track down the two people in the attached photo. I hasten to add that they are not in any trouble, nor are they suspected of having committed a crime. However, I believe that they might be able to help me to track the movements of a young woman in June 2016, a lady who became the victim of a major crime a few weeks ago. Please get in touch with me if you recognise either the man or the woman in the photo.
Yours faithfully,
Sam Gibb (Inquiry Agent)

After a number of days of radio silence, Gibb had almost given up hope of receiving a positive response. This morning, checking her inbox at the unearthly hour of half past six, a reply had arrived from Barry and Sara Kenton, a couple who ran an art studio from their home in North London. They had apologised for the delay in replying, but they had been visiting an exhibition in South America. Jennings's eyes had lit up when Gibb mentioned this particular snippet of information.

"Colombia? Bogotá?"

"No. Alas. Argentina. This isn't a Bev Bronte novel, David. Easily made connections, neat solutions and swift closure rarely happen in the real world. More's the pity. Still, we have an address and they'll be there all day. I've just spoken to them."

"Did you tell them what happened to Kate?"

"No. Lorna thinks that it's vital for you to talk to any of Kate's 'mystery people' face-to-face, and see how they react to the news. They may already know, of course. But either way, she wants you to 'read' their reaction. She also wants you to record the meeting on the little voice recorder she gave you yesterday. That way you can plug it into your USB tonight, upload the WAV/audio file and she can listen back to it."

Gibb had given him a street address – Cromwell Avenue – and was on the point of offering directions from the nearest Tube station when Jennings had interrupted her. He knew the tree-lined street intimately. It was another of his ghost roads. When Anne and he had moved in together more than twenty years ago, it had been into a two bedroom ground floor flat on Cromwell Avenue, a winding, residential street linking Highgate Hill with the busy Archway Road. History, connections and echoes. Jennings looked out of the train window. The Sussex countryside had made way for London suburbia: rows of terraced houses and satellite dishes, no doubt with startling price tags at odds with the modest, colourless architecture.

The Kenton's house was one of the few three storey buildings which hadn't been converted into flats. Barry was tall and skinny, with sunken cheeks and a shock of white hair. His wife had a similarly slight build, her coloured, reddish hair showing grey at the roots. Their gallery took up the entire attic space, a generous number of skylights letting in plenty of natural light. It had the scale of a loft but the artistic squalor of a cramped Parisian garret. Multi-coloured flecks of paint covered the linoleum floor, like an immense, modernist piece of art. A couple of life-sized human sculptures leaned against the walls, as if they were languid artists reposing. There was a raised platform in the centre of the room, with a couch on it. Sara explained that they took in art degree students, offered practical lessons and had weekly painting classes. They were clearly upset when Jennings told them about his daughter's death. They explained that she had answered their internet advertisement, the previous May, and had visited the house twice for evening art classes. They hadn't got to know her well, but both times she had stayed for a coffee and a chat about artists they mutually admired.

"I don't understand. Kate loved looking at art, but she never showed any interest in making it." Sara smiled, while gently shaking her head.

"Mr. Jennings – Kate wasn't here to paint. She was *painted*. She worked for us, as an artist's model."

"A *nude* model," Barry felt obliged to add.

"She posed as a nude model? Up here?" Jennings was stunned. He looked around the room, found his gaze focusing on the raised area, as if half-expecting to see her lying there. He found this revelation so out of character as to be almost unbelievable. Barry was shuffling towards a canvas on the far wall. He picked it up and brought it back over. It was a striking likeness of Kate, who was lying curled up – almost like a foetus – on a bright red sheet. She had a slim physique, but was far from the emaciated figure Jennings had been shown at the mortuary. He hadn't seen her without any clothes on since he used to bath Kate and Peter as little children. Now, in the space of two weeks, he had seen her naked twice: once in the flesh, dead; now on canvas, startlingly alive. Barry and Sara shared a look before the husband held out the painting to Jennings, no words required as the gift was offered.

"Did Kate come here on her own?"

"Yes –"

"No," Sara corrected him. "My husband has a wonderful artist's eye, but a shocking memory. Both times she arrived with an older woman. Auburn-haired. Plump-ish. At first I wondered if it was her mother, but I sensed that she was more confidante than mummy. As soon as the art students assembled, she left. Both times."

"I bow to Sara's far better memory. I was probably concentrating on the staging and light. We were looking to recreate a *fin-de-siècle* atmosphere. Wilde Paris, we called it, didn't we dear?"

"*You* did, yes."

****

Jennings was standing against a wall in the ticketing hall of a Tube station on the Northern Line. He was speaking to Lorna Myers, explaining about the modelling.

"This was completely out of character? You're absolutely sure?"

"Yes…No, not one hundred percent sure. I find it hard to fit the Kate I knew with this, but I'm beginning to understand what Graham Miles meant about strangers. I still think it's odd, though."

"What about asking Anne?"

"Jesus, Lorna! I told you about our horrendous soirée."

"Kate lived with Anne, not you. Surely she's in a better position to decide?"

"Yes." He sighed. "OK, I'll phone her now. See if she'll meet up for a coffee, on neutral territory."

"David, you make it sound like a Le Carré novel. Tread sensitively. Think you can manage that?"

****

The champagne-socialist side of David Jennings had always looked down on West Hampstead. In his student days it had been full of bedsits and young couples jumping on the property ladder, drawn in to a non-descript area of London by the misleading 'Hampstead' label. Now there seemed to be far more life about it and a burgeoning coffee shop culture. The owners of Wired Co. seemed to have the same enthusiasm for the origins and flavours of their beans as any small, independent wine merchant. Anne had ordered a flat white blend and Jennings had followed suit. It was delicious, a world away from the tasteless, grey drink British Rail used to offer when he was making away trips to watch his football team in the years after Anne and he had first met.

"I'll give you two things. One, you've got a fucking nerve dragging me out here after the other night. Two, you chose a good coffee shop."

"I'm sorry, Anne. I was completely out of order. I shouldn't have said that – about you wanting to move on."

"No, you bloody well shouldn't have. Do you think it's been easy? I'm not just talking about the last few days. When you left for Singapore, the children were distraught. What was I meant to say to them? Ten year olds don't understand concepts such as 'good career move'. They do understand what running away means, though."

"Is that what you told them?"

"I told them that you were still Daddy, but that Marcus would be their second Daddy. And he has been. Peter was fine, after the first few weeks. Kate – well, she was always the complicated one, wasn't she? You were her favourite, she was yours. Something died inside her when you left."

"Don't!"

"Don't what? Speak the truth? You put yourself ahead of our children, David, thus violating rule number one of parenthood. If you'd waited until they were eighteen, sixteen even, then fair enough."

"I know. I know." He felt close to tears. "I couldn't stand the Mrs. Doubtfire weekends. Trying to cram everything with them into a few hours."

"That was always your problem. They didn't need a child entertainer. Or whistle-stop tours around London. They just needed you. You know what I think? Kate choosing London and Literature, it was all about following in Daddy's footsteps. Despite you abandoning her. That's the difference. She never abandoned you. Always stood up for you, even when I slagged you off after one too many glasses of wine."

"And Marcus?"

"Marcus said nothing, simply watched on in silence. Like the other night. He never liked arguments."

"Going into the wrong profession then, isn't he?"

"You haven't heard? He hasn't been selected by the party. And no, before you ask, it had nothing to do with the hornets' nest you're trying to stir up. Talking of which…"

"I've still got people helping me look in to Kate's suicide." Anne raised her eyebrows, asking Jennings to offer more detail. "A policeman, the inquiry agent, that journalist, and now a profiler."

"Why not a butcher, baker and candlestick maker as well? Jesus, David! What are you trying to do? Dig up a demon?"

"If there is one, then yes."

"What if there isn't one? What if Kate had just...given up? What if she simply fell out of love with life?"

"I need to know."

"And now you want to drag me into your investigations?" Jennings nodded, bent down to pick up the canvas, looking around at the other customers. Everyone seemed busy with their screens: typing, scrolling, tucked away in their virtual worlds, oblivious to the middle-aged couple sitting in the corner, about to look at a nude painting of their recently dead daughter.

****

The revelation of the painting had been as much of a shock to Anne as it had been for him. She couldn't believe that her stubborn but shy daughter had posed nude in a room full of strangers. Kate had a part-time job in a local pub and a generous allowance from Marcus and Anne. She didn't need the extra cash and her life-style was a modest, almost frugal one. Then again, she had paid for a trip to Bogotá. Where had the money for that come from? The Colombia adventure had come as another complete surprise to her mother. Jennings was not the only one discovering that he had not known Kate nearly as well as he thought.

Jennings made the adjustment to his board. He printed off a small image of the nude painting as a replacement for the photo of the Kentons. Neither he nor Anne had known what to do with the original canvas. She had explained that Barry 'Baz' Kenton's art had been popular among the North London set for a brief period in the 1990s. Some of his paintings still fetched a decent price. Selling it was obviously out of the question. However, so too was hanging it in the living room at either Hampstead or Singapore. Anne took it back to her studio, where it would be covered in a dust sheet.

Lorna Myers was disturbed by the confirmation that the nude modelling was 'out of character'. She could only think of a single possible explanation. She recalled meeting Lee Kramer, a strikingly handsome but introverted young gay man, in Manhattan a few years back. He had been the victim of a drugged date rape by two older men. He reacted by posing nude for a photo shoot in a pink magazine. Why? Kramer had told her that it was a 'brutal' but carefully thought out decision. He wanted to expose his violated body in front of a mass audience, hoping that the feral rapists would see the pictures in the magazine. He told Myers that it was the hardest thing he had ever done, but that it had been a 'liberating' experience. If a similar, savage attack had been launched on Kate Jennings, then the modelling sessions had not had the same type of positive effect. Lorna Myers cursed. There she was again, thinking about 'types'. That was profiling for you. These were individual human beings she was talking about – both the victims and the sick bastards who had raped them.

There were so many myths (and misinformation) surrounding sexual violence, and these simply reinforced the sense of shame, self-blame and guilt which the battered women – and sometimes men – suffered. Often in silence. Alone. Cities like London were full of unknown and unknowable perils. Back in New York, single women were constantly warned to be vigilant when walking the city streets, particularly late at night. 'Stranger Danger'. Yet Myers knew that 90% of rapes were committed by men who were known, often trusted. It was about violence and control. Not desire. The clichéd excuses were always inexcusable: 'Sometimes no means yes'; 'She led me on'; 'I'd had too much to drink.' She had heard them all. Particularly where alcohol was involved and used by defence attorneys as a mitigating factor. Bullshit! It was the attacker who committed the crime, not the bottle of bourbon.

If Kate had been raped – and it was still an 'if' – then she clearly hadn't reported it to the police. That would have been picked up by the coroner's inquest. Myers knew that she could share the Lee Kramer story with Jennings, but would it do any good? After all, it was simply a vague connection, a theoretical possibility. Nothing more. Perhaps Kate had sought out specialist counselling, or even attended therapeutic group sessions. She would ask Sam to investigate these first, before broaching the subject with Jennings. The man was suffering enough already. For now it was conjecture, unnecessary information. Worse still, harrowing *mis*information.

Meanwhile, Sam Gibb had received a piece of genuine information about the clinic photograph. Except that it was non-information so far as Kate Jennings was concerned. The building in the picture was a GPs group practice in North London and Kate had not been a patient there. Perhaps the auburn-haired lady was, and Jennings's daughter had been accompanying her to a stressful appointment. There was no way of finding out. The woman was now the only unknown person in the jigsaw, but was remaining stubbornly untraceable. Gibb sensed that it was time to investigate the other mystery.

Carolina González had shared a flat with Kate for eight months. She had been studying Sociology at the London School of Economics. That much the inquiry agent had been able to unearth. Why, though, had she suddenly abandoned both and returned to Bogotá? And why had Kate travelled out there four months later? The two mature students had been unable to offer an explanation. The LSE had, naturally, refused to provide any more information about her. She sensed that Vince Harrison's journalist card would simply result in more drawbridges being pulled up. It was time to ring DI Miles, and plead a very big favour.

ELEVEN

Graham Miles' investigations often took him far outside the Brighton and Hove area. However, London was new, unfamiliar territory. Common sense had told him to reject Sam Gibb's dulcet tones. He had no right to barge into an academic institution in the capital, demanding information. If it all went Pete Tong then he could be looking at a written warning from his Chief Constable. However, cautionary common sense had played third fiddle to gut instinct and an inbuilt moral sense of duty throughout his thirty years on the Sussex Police force.

Alighting at Covent Garden Tube, Miles made his way through the Clare Market district. He seemed to be surrounded by law and order: the Royal Courts of Justice, Lincoln's Inn. He vaguely recalled that the LSE had been at the centre of controversy a few years back, something to do with alleged links to the Libyan regime of Muammar Gaddafi. He couldn't remember the exact circumstances, nor what the outcome had been. He had googled directions for the LSE, noting that its Latin motto translated as 'To Know the Causes of Things', which seemed fitting, given the mission he was on. Wasn't that what David Jennings wanted? As a father himself, he would have been striving for the same thing.

Sixty something, well-upholstered, wearing a royal blue trouser suit, Margery Henderson, the lady who he was sent to in the student records office, reminded him of a frosty librarian. Perhaps it was impossible for anyone to spend all day on a computer terminal, simply updating and collating facts, without losing their human touch.

"Carolina González. Presumably here on a student visa. She would have enrolled in the autumn of 2014. She was studying Sociology."

"And what precisely did you want to know about her, Mr –"

"Miles." He pulled his black warrant card out. "DI Miles." The woman's eyes expressed mild panic, seemingly unsure where to look – at Miles, his identification card or back at her computer terminal. This common reaction had always mildly amused him. Even the most law-abiding citizen couldn't help but behave in a shifty manner when the card was produced. It created a moment of dramatic edginess. It reminded Miles of his school days, whenever the head teacher had stood in front of the assembled pupils, after an escalated outbreak of vandalism or bullying. You felt an irrational sense of guilt, or the imminent arrival of a fit of giggles, even though you hadn't done anything wrong. Once, after a teacher's bag had gone missing and no one had owned up, he had almost put his hand up to 'confess' to the theft, such was the discomfort in the assembly hall. Authority figures could do that to you.

He didn't feel guilty about flashing his I.D. in front of her. He knew police officers who took serious liberties with their warrant cards: blagging free first class train travel, entrance to bars and clubs, pulling it out at road rage incidents in their private vehicles, even during heated disputes with their neighbours. 'I'm a copper, I can do what I like', seemed to be the message. Well, nowadays you could be sacked on the spot for that sort of thing. Was he abusing his position now? Yes, but the motive was a selfless, honourable one. Not that it would necessarily wash with his ACC. Ms. Henderson had gone to fetch her boss. When he arrived, moments later, he looked flushed, tugging at his tie to loosen it, while attempting to maintain his dignity and poise.

"DI Miles, please come through into the office." Miles tried a smile at the retreating Margery, before deciding that it would be easier to melt an iceberg than win a similar response from the elderly admin clerk. Colin Simmons asked to see Miles' warrant card, making a show of studying it closely. "You're a long way from Sussex, Detective Inspector."

"We think that Carolina González's sudden disappearance may be connected to a case we are looking into in Brighton, sir. One involving another London-based student."

"Disappearance?" Simmons clicked onto the student's file. "Carolina González: she was about half way through her three year degree, withdrew from her Sociology course in April last year. 'Disappearance' is a rather dramatic way to describe it, don't you think? According to our records she simply returned home. There are always a few undergraduates dropping out. It's not unusual. Particularly for a young woman thousands of miles from home."

"With any investigation we have to keep an open mind, Mr. Simmons. Explore every line of inquiry. It's a bit like your motto here."

"'Rerum *cognoscere causas*'? It's Virgil, Book 2 of the Georgics."

"'Always seek out the cause'. It's Miles, Book 1 of police life." Simmons smiled, beginning to accept defeat.

"What information do you want me to give you, DI Miles?"

"The modules she took, essay and exam grades, names of her tutors, closest relatives to contact in an emergency, passport number, home address back in Colombia." Simmons put his hand up.

"Why don't I just give you everything we've got?" He began to print off all of Carolina González's details.

****

Jennings and Vince Harrison were standing in the Hove studio flat, the journalist nodding approvingly at the board.

"Lorna thinks you should go out to Colombia?" Jennings nodded. Lorna Myers had gone much further, suggesting that this was probably the only route left to complete Kate's puzzle. "Well, Bogotá is a lot safer than it was twenty years ago. But this address is in the Ciudad Bolivar."

"Do you know it?"

"Oh yes. It's where I did most of my research for the article I wrote. It's the largest, poorest, and most violent *barrio* in the city. In the country."

"Great!"

"If you're serious about going out there then you'll need a guide. And a crash course on Colombian culture and politics. I'll ring my friend Javier Garcia. He speaks fluent English, studied over here. A bit of a ladies' man! He's a lecturer in the city, and someone at the heart of social reform. If he can spare the time then there's no one better to take you there. It's not safe to travel to that part of the city on your own. As for the crash course, I'll offer you what I know over dinner. English's? I've got a craving for some oysters."

English's was a seafood restaurant and oyster bar near the seafront, in the heart of the Lanes. Formerly three fishermen's cottages, it was something of a Brighton institution. They both plumped for the set menu, Jennings ordering the mussels, cider and shallot cream as a starter, followed by fillet of seabass, artichoke purée and roasted garlic in a red wine sauce. Taking a slurp from his glass of house white, he sat back while Harrison told him about one of the most contradictory and complex countries in the world.

"If you think India is *the* diverse country of extremes, think again. Colombia has it all. To begin with, it has almost every possible landscape known to man: Caribbean coastline, coral reefs, rainforests, dramatic hilltops and mountain ranges, desert, unpopulated lowlands. It's in the Ring of Fire, so add earthquakes and volcanic eruptions. There are towns and villages frozen in time, ancient, 'lost' cities accessed through jungle which are straight out of a Tintin comic."

"It sounds stunning."

"It is. But then again, it's suffered the longest continuous war in the world – a four-sided civil war involving narcotic cartels, right-wing paramilitaries, guerrilla revolutionaries, and the government army. Millions displaced, violence from gangs and the police. For every gold artefact dug up, there's a mass grave unearthed. *La Violencia*. It can strike anywhere, from remote areas to crowded streets. There's been a concerted effort to bring peace and a fairer society, but reform is fiendishly complicated. Not easy to manage ceasefires, a rural reform of land rights, an end to cocaine production. How do you create a framework in which every side can participate politically, including gangsters and terrorists? This is a country which has almost everything – mineral fuels, oils, coffee, sugar...but where there are millions of people with nothing. People forced to abandon their rural homes for life in the lower *barrios*. I don't want you to think of Ciudad Bolivar as a heart of darkness. Most of the residents just want a chance to live in peace. But you need to be prepared for a culture shock, and be aware of some of the dangers of stepping inside."

"*Some?*"

"No one even knows how many people there are living there. 700,000? A million? Two? It's one of the largest mega-slums on the planet. And yet, while standing there amidst this unimaginable density of people – who live alongside violence and murder – I felt, strangely, that it's also a place full of hope. There's a real sense of community. David, when I went there for the first time, Javier warned me that you need to expect everything, anything...and nothing."

****

Sam Gibb had arranged the flights: British Airways from London Heathrow to Madrid; Iberia to Bogotá's El Dorado International Airport. Harrison had recommended that he stay in a genuine Colombian hotel, rather than one of the hundreds of characterless high rise ones which catered for business people and tourists. The Tip Top Casa Hotel was located in the *Centro Historico*, barely two hundred yards from the Gold Museum. Myers felt that it was important to visit it while he was there, reminding Jennings that places were just as important as people in Kate's jigsaw. Javier Garcia would be meeting him at the hotel, and taking him in to the Ciudad Bolivar the following day.

Jennings had always enjoyed foreign travel. As a child his parents had taken him to Portugal, Spain, and France. He loved the different smells, the sound of other languages being spoken like rapid fire, the unfamiliar fruits and vegetables for sale in bustling markets, and the chance to try strange new dishes in restaurants. Over the past ten years, he had discovered the Maghreb region of North Africa, particularly drawn to Morocco. He was fascinated by the exotic mixture of Persian, Islamic and Mediterranean architecture: the mosaics, arches, domes, roof tiles, calligraphy, arabesque decorations and geometric patterns. The clay walls of the houses backing on to the narrow streets were a mass of vibrant colours and textures, but their windowless façades hid the treasures waiting for you when you entered a *riad*. He always opted to stay in one of these, gazing out at the city's maze of rooftops from the terrace and spending hours reading in the shade of its central atrium courtyard. He loved the buildings' inward focus, the reflective peace and quiet. It offered a wonderful contrast to the early morning journeying into the heart of a busy souk, bazaar or spice market. He found the people friendly, polite and gentle, often happy to welcome him into their homes and serve him *atai*, a green tea which seemed to represent both an art form and the symbol of hospitality. A couple of years ago he had met a lecturer in Moroccan literature who had introduced him to some exciting contemporary fiction and home-made Moorish cuisine. Despite the Marrakesh professor speaking fluent English, it had been a rare opportunity to use his French.

Colombia would be very different. This wasn't a holiday or cultural exchange. If he was being honest, it was the act of a desperate man. Someone drowning, on the point of giving up hope. A mad, final attempt to make sense of the last few weeks. The last twenty years. Lorna Myers had tried to reassure him that the trip was important. If he didn't go, he would forever wonder, 'What if?' Perhaps Carolina González could shed light on what had happened in both Kate's life and in her mind. Vince Harrison had told him that the country was far safer than it used to be. Nevertheless, as he packed his suitcase and prepared to leave for the airport hotel, he couldn't help but think that he was chasing shadows, or rainbows.

He would be out of his comfort zone. He had never visited South America and couldn't speak a word of Spanish. The three day trip promised to take him further than ever from the world he knew and understood. Understood? Who was he kidding? Kate's suicide had already shattered any sense of a knowable world.

As he travelled by taxi to the station he recalled Javier Garcia's warning: he should expect everything, anything and nothing.

TWELVE

It was 16:35 local time when Jennings's Iberia flight touched down at Bogotá's international airport. However, with Colombia being five hours behind, his body clock felt that it was already mid-evening. "Welcome to El Dorado," the Iberia stewardess said to him. He remembered Harrison's comment that some people referred to the legend as a person, not a lost city. Well, he could identify with that. Javier Garcia had organised a taxi to take him to the hotel in Candelaria, fourteen kilometres away. It was a mild, sunny afternoon, and the grey-haired driver, Carlos, told him that he was lucky – spring had arrived early. Jennings commented on how heavy the traffic was.

"Señor, this is normal! Since 1950s, no public transport except for buses. My father remembers trams here, but they stopped when he was a boy, soon after *El Bogotazo*. The riots. Then the trains shut when *I* was at school."

"Is there no metro?"

"They say there will be. In four or five years' time. Who knows? They have talked about building it since the tram closed. Politicians are good at talking, eh?" Jennings laughed and agreed. "My sister lives in Medellin. Medellin has *three* metro lines and even metro-cables, but we have no lines, just talk. This city is three times bigger than Medellin but we have nothing, just eight million people trying to cross it! Welcome to Bogotá, Señor."

The taxi dropped him off in front of the small hotel, its façade a vibrant mishmash of colours – yellows, blues and greens. The inside was equally quirky, with a delightful jumble of furniture, floor tiles, glass atriums, galleries and oddly shaped windows and doors. Having taken a shower in his room, Jennings made his way up to the rooftop terrace. The surrounding buildings were an interesting mixture of sizes, heights and styles. The *Centro Historico* was overlooked by the impressive Guadalupe Hills. He was glad that he had taken up Harrison's suggestion, rather than staying in a characterless, chain hotel. Instead of international businessmen or tourists, the Tip Top Casa felt like the sort of place where you might bump into someone reading Alex Garland's *The Beach*, or even a character from it.

Javier Garcia's handshake was firm but friendly. He was a tall, naturally elegant man who still looked smart dressed in a linen jacket and jeans. His black moustache had flecks of grey in it, but Jennings imagined that even these would add to his physical appeal. He apologised that he was smoking and stubbed the cigarette out in one of the ceramic table ashtrays. The light had already faded from the early evening sky and the night air was cold. Garcia suggested a local restaurant where they could chat in the warmth.

Restaurante Fulanitos served traditional Colombian food in a beautiful old colonial house. Garcia recommended the *sancocho trifásico* which he said was a soup. They ordered and settled back.

"Hungry, David?" Had he heard Jennings's stomach rumbling? "Don't worry. Think stew, not soup. It is an entire meal in a bowl. I will be surprised if you are disappointed. Tell me something about your daughter. Kate?"

"I don't know where to start."

"What were her passions? I hate that English expression 'hobbies'. It's so cold a word. It sounds like dull activities thought up to fill the hours on a wet Sunday afternoon."

"Kate loved discovering new cities. And languages. And going for walks in the countryside. She devoured books, architecture, sculpture, history – as long as it dealt with normal people rather than kings and queens. She loved eating out, and cooking, particularly French cuisine."

"Why does someone with so much to live for decide *not* to live?"

"That's what I can't understand. Something terrible must have happened to her. I'm hoping this girl, Carolina González, may be able to help me to understand." The food arrived. Garcia grinned as Jennings's eyes visibly widened.

"*Sancocho trifásico*. This is Sunday lunch in a Colombian home. Well, in my mother's anyway. *Trifásico* – three meats. I think we have chicken, beef cuts and pig's feet. Potatoes, yuca, onions, garlic cloves, red pepper, corn, and green plantains. Achiote, cumin, cilantro – it's from the same plant as coriander, but a very different flavour. We always serve it with a side dish of avocado, white rice and a hot sauce – *aji picante*. Enjoy!" It simply wasn't possible for Jennings to talk at any length while devouring this incredible dish. Also, he wasn't sure where to begin as he had so many questions that he wanted to put to Garcia.

"Our friend Vince is well?"

"Yes. Although I don't know how he functions on almost no sleep. He seems to survive on caffeine, nicotine and missions to right wrongs. He told me that you're an Urbanology expert, but I have to confess that I don't really know what that is. I quickly googled it and it sounded like a cross between city planning and sociology."

"In a way I suppose it is. We try to place ourselves at the heart of the debate on urban development. I don't want to sit in an office or institute all the time. I directly engage with places and people: residents as well as architects and planners."

"You've been involved with the Ciudad Bolivar?"

"Yes. The first thing you need to know about it is that the Ciudad Bolivar is impossible to understand fully. You also have to ignore most things which politicians and journalists say about the place. Officially, about one in every ten people in the city lives there. The truth is that it is probably closer to one in four. We have a massive problem in this country, a historical situation in which five million people were displaced, either forced to leave their land or attracted by the American Dream of the big city lights. These rural immigrants arrived in Bogotá and were unable to afford to buy a home. So they began to build homes in the 19th district with their own hands. Simple houses constructed of bricks and metal sheeting or whatever they could find. No proper foundations or sanitation. And when the family grows, they simply add another floor. These are desperate people. They don't care about not legally owning the land, or whether there are environmental hazards and geological instability."

"You said that the place is incomprehensible. In what way?"

"For one thing, the sheer scale of the place. Ciudad Bolivar is a *city* on the edge of our city. Maybe two million people. And then there is the density. I remember visiting New York for a conference once. A colleague from Paris was complaining over lunch one day about how claustrophobic she found it. New York has less than ten thousand people per square kilometre; many of the townships of the Ciudad Bolivar have more than forty thousand! Of course there will be bloodshed and warfare when people are packed in like caged beasts."

"What is the government doing about it?"

"They are gradually legalising the settlements, but it is a nightmarish task. We are talking about hundreds of thousands of houses built without plans or permits. Then there is the cost of retrofitting homes for phone lines and sanitation. Most of the residents work, but in the 'informal market'."

"On the black…illegally?"

"Yes. Half this country works 'on the black'. The government would rather offer them new plots, already connected to basic amenities. But these people cannot afford them! It is a vicious circle."

"You mentioned journalists."

"Yes. They come from all over the country. From across the globe. And they only skim the surface and the statistics. They know that this is the third largest 'mega-slum' in the world. That there is one police station for every 100,000 people. They note that assault is the first cause of death in the *barrio*. They are not interested in delving deeper. They simply reinforce the stigma."

"Including Vince?"

"Vince is a good man. A close friend. But even he came to research a negative story: drug gangs, assassinations, street kids."

"And now I arrive to look in to my daughter's suicide."

"That is very different, David – yours is a tragic, private matter. But tomorrow, try to keep an open mind about our city-within-the-city. When we head in to Cordillera, look out for the other side to Ciudad Bolivar. Neighbours happily chatting in the streets, children playing – despite the lack of green spaces. See how many people have converted their ground floor into workspaces and small businesses. Watch the thousands of men returning home from jobs on building sites or in factories. There are internet cafés springing up, and *malokas* – community buildings where people can meet to chat, share ideas, fears, knowledge and information. In Urbanology, we call somewhere like Ciudad Bolivar an 'informal settlement', not a slum. These places are not a temporary problem. They are not going to disappear. They are the future for many huge cities. We have to work with the settlements and the settlers, not stigmatise them. OK. Lecture over. How was your journey? How do you like our food? Is your hotel room comfortable?" Both men laughed, before sharing a joke about chatty taxi drivers. Whether it was Charlie Smith driving a black cab in London, or Carlos Rojas in charge of a battered old Mercedes in Bogotá, it seemed that taxi driver rants were a global phenomenon: these men could talk you to death while remaking the world.

THIRTEEN

Jennings stood at the top of the hillside, staring down at a mass of brick and metal sheeting. When they had arrived at the edge of the Cordillera district, Garcia had pointed out that they would have to continue on foot. It soon became obvious why. There were no streets, just a labyrinth of dusty paths which – like the buildings – made their way haphazardly up to the summit of the surrounding hills. Some of the houses looked half-built, or half-demolished. Others were surprisingly elaborate three storey constructions. Some had dull brick façades, while others were gaily painted. The people they had passed were, for the most part, wary but polite. Garcia had observed that street names and zip codes had little meaning here. Eventually he had stopped at one of the communal shelters for a glass of water and directions.

The house they were now standing outside was a two storey building, painted pale green. The upper floor hung over what must have originally been a single storey dwelling. Standing next to Garcia was a short, elderly woman with thick grey hair and a bowed back. Her voice was weak but her arms moved about excitedly as she engaged in what seemed to be an animated, fairly one-sided conversation with Garcia. Eventually she stopped talking, went back inside, and he came across to Jennings.

"Señora González is Carolina's grandmother. She says that Carolina is at work, in the city and that she won't be back until this evening. She wants us to come inside for a coffee."

Maria González was hunched over a stove, heating a small pan. With the front door left open there was plenty of natural light inside. The ground floor was one room. The area around the stove was tiled, but the remainder was bare earth. There was no electricity or water, although there was a makeshift fireplace.

Jennings imagined that at night-time, even with a candle lit or the fire blazing, the interior must be like a damp cave. They drank coffee out of tiny ceramic cups, and Garcia offered an instant translation as the old lady spoke.

"The Señora is a widow. She runs an unofficial after-school nursery for children whose parents are at work. Her husband was a farmer and they lived in the Andean highlands. Their people are the Muisca. Señor González was as stubborn as a donkey, by all accounts. He spoke Chibcha and refused to talk to people in Spanish. One day their land was seized by local mafia and they were told to leave. When the senor refused, they shot him dead and gave the family an hour to pack. They moved here in the 1980s with the husband's two surviving brothers. The two men built the house. When Carolina's father reached fourteen he found a job in a factory. Her mother was a health worker in the *barrio*."

"*Was?*"

"They were killed in 2001, shot dead as they walked home together. It was a local drug addict, needing money to pay his supplier. Maria brought her granddaughter up. Says that Carolina is an angel. Her guardian angel. She came back from England because 'bad things happened'. Maria doesn't know anything more. She has never asked. Carolina works at –"

"I understood that bit – *El Museo del Oro* – the Gold Museum."

****

Jennings immediately recognised the front entrance to the museum from Kate's photo. Even if he hadn't, the name was stylishly picked out in glazed lettering on its white-washed concrete exterior. It was a strikingly modernist, three storey building, though dwarfed by the two high-rise blocks behind it. Carolina worked in the souvenir shop and café on the ground floor. On the return journey from the

Ciudad Bolivar, Garcia had commented that the Gold Museum was an appropriate place for Carolina González to work. Perhaps it had been a deliberate choice.

"It celebrates the cultures which existed here in pre-Hispanic times. The Muisca people were one of the great civilizations, like the Aztecs, Mayas and Incas. The museum has the biggest collection of gold in the world, but it is the Muisca Raft which is the centrepiece."

"The El Dorado Raft?"

"The same. It is an extraordinary piece of art, whatever else it may be. The Spanish Conquistadors sought out a city of gold, because they were motivated by greed. But the Muisca were happy to make elaborate objects out of their gold and then throw them away into a secret, sacred lake, as spiritual offerings. Who was right?" Javier Garcia shrugged, as if telling Jennings to make his own mind up. "You must see the raft. It's on the third floor. In the Offering Room. It may help you to understand Carolina's family history, her roots. It may even help you to make sense of our crazy country! *Then* we will find Señorita González."

Before travelling out to Colombia, Jennings had watched a short documentary on *YouTube* in which an artisan had demonstrated how the 'lost wax technique' could enable you to create a metal sculpture, using a clay mould. Jennings was not a practical man and his eyes had soon glazed over as the process was explained. Nevertheless, it was clearly a painstakingly drawn-out procedure and the dedicated work of a master craftsman. The Muisca Raft was a votive figure, an offering. It was created for a ceremony – the initiation and investiture of a new chief or *zipa*. The man would cover his body in gold dust and jump into the sacred lake, taking with him gold and emerald offerings.

It was an extraordinary object. The base was the shape of a log boat and there were various figures on the raft. Naturally, the *zipa* was the central figure and by far the largest one. He was decorated in headdresses, nose rings and earrings. Some of the others looked like soldiers, but carried banners, canes and masks. Were the ones on the edges of the log raft rowers? The Muisca Raft had an indescribable aura about it. You instantly and instinctively felt that it was far more than a piece of art. It demanded to be interpreted. Jennings felt that it represented something which he would never be able to understand fully. The ceramic container which it had been found in depicted a shaman sitting in the thinking position. The Raft might have been an offering, but it also seemed to symbolise a life of quiet, contemplative reflection, a retreat from a world of brutal warfare and conquest. There was something paradoxical and puzzling about it, a haunting beauty, and the sense of both a place and time which had vanished. Yet this particular piece had been unearthed by three farmers in a cave, an extraordinary discovery of a lost past, frozen in gold, copper and silver. It was almost as if its power had attracted them to it, like a golden magnet. Fate, rather than chance. Jennings was mesmerised.

An hour later, David Jennings, Javier Garcia and Carolina González sat drinking coffee in a small café in the historical district. Carolina already knew about Kate. She was visibly upset the first time Jennings mentioned her name. He had quickly changed the focus of the conversation, asking her to tell them about her time in England.

The opportunity to study in London had come thanks to Jorge, her great uncle, one of the men who fled the Andean farmhouse when the mafia men shot dead his brother. He was a blacksmith, and dragged some of the tools of his trade hundreds of miles to the Ciudad Bolivar. In their new makeshift home he created a new forge in a crude metal outbuilding. Jorge never married and treated both Carolina and her mother as if they were his own offspring. When the mother was also killed, he promised Maria González that he would find a way out of the *barrio* for the little girl. A family friend was living in London, working in the kitchens at restaurants such as La Bodeguita, El Rancho De Lalo and Donde Carlos. Through a network of fellow immigrants he found a house full of Colombian students with a spare room which Carolina could live in, and the offer of part-time work as a waitress. The LSE was one of the best institutions in the world to study Urban Sociology. In the first year, the course had gone well, but she had major problems with the landlord. The house was infested with vermin and the toilet and shower did not work properly. The man promised on a number of occasions to get these fixed but never did. One night Carolina woke to the sight and smell of a rat nesting in her bed and decided that she needed to move. By chance, or fate – that word again! – that same weekend she had agreed to meet a fellow Colombian student in a tapas bar. The girl never turned up and the waitress asked her if she would mind sharing a table with another young woman. Kate.

They had clicked straight away, chatting animatedly about their studies, families and shared interests such as World Cinema. By the end of the evening Kate had asked her if she would like to move in to the four-bedroom flat which three of them had visited and secured that afternoon.

"The two of you became good friends?"

"Best friends".

"What went wrong?" Carolina looked at Jennings blankly. "You abandoned your course, the flat, your new life in England. Your grandmother said that something bad happened but that you didn't tell her what." She immediately reverted to Spanish, looking away as she spoke.

"Mi abuela es muy mayor. Ella se preocupa demasiado por mi. No podía decírselo. Y no puedo decírtelo." She shook her head, while tears ran down her cheeks. Jennings felt torn apart. He didn't want to twist a knife into whatever raw wound someone had inflicted on Carolina. However, he had come so far and this girl was his last chance. He felt that now, as never before.

FOURTEEN

It took Jennings the best part of a day to recover physically from the flight and the highland climate of Bogotá. The trip had provided some life-affirming memories, in particular experiencing the Ciudad Bolivar and the Muisca Raft first hand. However, there were also emotional scars, ones which he sensed would never fully heal. In forcing Carolina to relive her night-time experience near Highgate Hill, another piece of the jigsaw puzzle had been explained, but the added knowledge was decidedly bitter. Sam Gibb's warning at their first meeting had echoed in his mind a number of times on the return plane journey: "And if we do reach a conclusion, what if the truth turns out to be worse than not knowing?"

Soon after Carolina González moved into Kate's student flat, the two young women started waitressing at a gastro pub on Highgate Hill. They worked the same evening shifts, three nights each week. The pub stopped serving food at ten and they would walk home together. The journey took about twelve minutes, downhill all the way. After a few months they had become familiar with the clientele, most of whom were locals. Generally speaking, the customers were polite and friendly, but there was one man, Johnny Holmes, who they both took an instant dislike to. He had a social arrogance about him which only a certain type of private school education can provide. He was a bar fly, arriving at around six o'clock, usually wearing a velvet or linen jacket, formal shirt and paisley cravat scarf. Cosmetically, he was, the girls both acknowledged, vaguely attractive, in a seedy way. However, it was a Dorian Gray veneer. In ten years' time he would simply be sleazy and he seemed to have inwardly acknowledged that. He flirted indiscriminately with all the student waitresses, at first in a seemingly playful way but – as the drink took its effect – his behaviour became charmless and desperate. There was something dead about his eyes. Or behind them. Mid-evening, his clothes would already look slept in, his receding blond hair greasy. By the time the two girls finished their shift, the stares he offered them were usually malevolent; there was a thinly-veiled threat in his unwholesome features. He was a sexual predator and had he spoken with an Estuary accent rather than the clipped voice of an Old Etonian, everyone would have seen him for what he was – dangerously feral. Instead, the landlord affectionately referred to him as 'harmless Johnny'. Occasionally he arrived on his own, but normally he was accompanied by a thick-set, shaven-headed older man who spoke with an Eastern European accent. Someone had told Carolina that he was Ukrainian. He looked like a bouncer or body builder and rarely spoke above a hoarse whisper. Neither man ever ordered food, but sat in silent conference at the bar, scanning the restaurant area for 'talent' while hoovering up any free bar snacks which appeared. None of the staff seemed to know what Holmes did for a living, nor what the connection was between the two men. He had once hinted to Kate that he was a record producer, but the two women found this unlikely. What had Kate said about the story? It was a tale told by an idiot in a bar, signifying nothing.

Johnny Holmes had developed the tedious habit of always offering the two of them a drink when they clocked off. Politely turned down on each occasion, he would sarcastically salute them as they made their way out. On one particular night, he had said nothing as they went out the front doors, seemingly oblivious that they were leaving. However, soon after starting their walk home, Carolina and Kate were aware that the two men were a hundred metres or so behind them. This was unusual. Holmes and his mate were creatures of habit, doggedly staying in the pub until closing time. At first the girls presumed that Holmes and the Ukrainian were simply heading in the same general direction. However, as they crossed the Archway Road both women suddenly, instinctively felt that something was very wrong. Carolina had glanced back twice, noting that both men were staring ahead at them. Following them. She and Kate increased their speed, finally breaking into a running walk. Then Kate noticed that the monkey was no longer there, only Johnny the organ grinder. It was the nickname the waitresses used for him, as his hand often rested on his groin area when he was speaking to any of them.

It was then that Kate made a decision which had nightmarish consequences. Unwilling to let him see where they lived, she took Carolina down a narrow, badly-lit passageway which connected two residential streets. Holmes was now less than thirty metres behind. As they turned a bend at the halfway point, they were immediately aware of the monkey standing ahead of them, his powerful, bulky silhouette illuminated by the sodium lighting. They were trapped. Carolina remembered thinking that not only would they be raped, but that their lives might be snuffed out. Holmes was making his way towards her, silently indicating to his partner that Kate was his. Neither woman said a word, or even screamed out. The scenario was so horribly surreal that rational, lucid thought ceased to function.

Carolina remembered seeing Kate simply standing there, passive, against the high brick wall which separated the passageway from people's back gardens. The monkey was pulling her shirt up. Why wasn't she putting up any resistance? Preparing for battle? It was as if she had resigned herself to being violated. You would not survive in the Ciudad Bolivar with that approach. Carolina looked Holmes in the eyes. His face was sweaty-drunk, barely able to focus his eyes on her. Nor was he physically strong. She launched herself at him, instinctively aiming a kick into the groin area. He bent over and started to moan with pain. She immediately followed this up sending her right knee into his face. He lay on the floor, barely conscious. She crouched down, biting him fully on the nose until she could feel the fine, rubbery cartilage snapping. She jumped back up and turned to face the other man. He had ripped Kate's top and bra off, pulled her trousers and pants down and was now removing his own clothes. Carolina drove her sharp nails into and down the man's back. She felt like a wild cat, digging its claws into the enemy in a territorial dispute to the death. As the man shrugged her off and turned to attack, Carolina screamed at Kate, before pulling out her pepper spray and aiming directly at his eyes. When the Ukrainian saw what she was holding, he turned his face away, but a fraction too late. He was soon coughing, spluttering and having difficulty breathing but Carolina stepped closer, continuing to spray until the man dropped to his knees. She even had the presence of mind to pull out her phone and take a series of photos of both of their assailants. She helped Kate put her clothes back on, her friend's face worryingly expressionless. Carolina was furious, her adrenalin pumping; she was almost tempted to relaunch her assault on the men, but Kate seemed to have retreated into a shell. It was as if she was, mentally, elsewhere. As a parting gesture, Carolina grabbed all of the Ukrainian's clothes and hurled them over the wall.

Looking back on the event, she could not recall the short walk home, apart from the constant need to guide Kate, as you might a sleepwalker. When they reached the flat, neither of them spoke for a few minutes. Carolina made them both a coffee and immediately realised that she needed to take charge, to control what happened next. Her hands were shaking so much that she spilt boiling water onto the laminate kitchen floor. The reality of what had just happened, and also what had so nearly taken place, had not fully sunk in. Instead, she was being driven by fury. She realised that her rage was not solely directed at the two men. Kate had done nothing to help them. How dare she just stand there, waiting to become a victim? What was wrong with her? Carolina should have phoned the police, she knew that. However, in the *barrio* you don't trust them. For every tale of gang violence or killing, there was one involving the police. Instead, she sent a text to her great uncle Jorge's restaurant friend. Told him what had happened, attached the photos. If the organ grinder and his monkey thought of themselves as mean bastards, they hadn't seen anything yet. Carolina didn't care if they simply received a beating, or suffered something far worse. It wasn't her problem anymore. Laws of the jungle. Survival of the fittest. She instinctively sensed that her dead parents would have been proud of her tonight, just as she knew that she could never tell her grandmother about what had occurred. She had also made her mind up – without being aware of there being a conscious decision – to leave London and return home.

Over the following two days Carolina was running around like the proverbial headless chicken, resigning from both her university degree course and job, organising a return flight, and saying her goodbyes to various Colombian friends and distant relatives. Kate locked herself away in her room, saying that she had an extended essay to write on Kate Chopin. On their final evening together the girls made some popcorn and watched one of their favourite films, *Ghost*. Both of them sobbed uncontrollably, just as they did whenever they pulled the romantic fantasy thriller off Kate's shelf. As the end credits finished, Carolina grasped Kate's hand and asked her to explain what had been happening inside her head forty-eight hours earlier.

"I just wanted it over with."

"You would have let him rape you?" Kate nodded. "You stood there like a lifeless…mannequin. I thought I knew you, but I can't understand this. Why not fight back, resist?" Kate had shed silent tears before looking at her best friend.

"Last time I *did* resist. And protest. It didn't stop him."

"'*Last time*'? You mean you've been attacked before?"

"I don't want to talk about it, Carolina. I managed to put it behind me. In that alleyway I had two choices: fight like you and bring those horrible memories back; or send my mind somewhere else and pretend that it wasn't happening." The two women hugged and Carolina decided not to ask her anything else about it. Everyone had a cupboard of bad dreams and you didn't always solve the problem by opening it and looking inside. While she had decided to fight in that alley, Kate had chosen flight. End of story.

Of course that wasn't an end to the story as far as Jennings was concerned. *Last time*. What had happened to Kate? When? Had she been raped? Who was her abuser? Was it someone she had known? Someone he knew?

Jennings lay in bed that night, listening to the waves once again. The sea was fairly calm tonight. His whirlwind trip to Bogotá already seemed like an event in the distant past. The manic traffic, early morning fog, his wonderful meal with Javier Garcia, the journey through the Ciudad Bolivar, meeting Maria González and then her granddaughter Carolina. What had Maria called her? A guardian angel. She had certainly been that for Kate, that night in a badly-lit alleyway. However, she had not been able to save her from a deeper wound, some dark memory which Kate buried in her subconscious mind, lying dormant until the assault unearthed it.

Jennings was chasing shadows, had been from the moment he decided to investigate his daughter's death. No, 'death' was almost a euphemism. Her *suicide*. He was still trying to tap into Kate's black box, read things which were hidden, concealed, repressed even. Would uncovering her abuser change anything? Would it make him feel any better? Had Kate really wanted someone unmasked? If so, why not simply leave a note explaining why she had chosen to take her own life, naming her abuser? Perhaps Anne was right, that his mission was both ridiculous and guilt-ridden.

He was trying to rewrite a fairy tale which he had created, but which had gone horribly wrong. Once upon a time, he had made a private Eden where he and his daughter could play happily ever after. He had even locked a loving wife out, unwilling to share his little princess with her. Then one fine day he simply walked away, abandoning their secret garden, breaking up their special relationship. He had left it to others to tend the lawn, pull up any weeds. If an ogre had climbed in, wasn't he at least partly responsible? He hadn't been there. He abandoned his children's universe and now he was trying to return to it. Too late, David. Kate blew that world apart weeks ago, and nothing can be achieved by looking around blindly for tiny fragments. It was like searching for lost time when the clock has stopped.

As Jennings drifted towards sleep he sensed that he was on the verge of abandoning his quest. He should be spending time with the child who was still living, not the one who had chosen to die. Hadn't he always favoured Kate? Did he never learn?

He felt strangely envious of Carolina González. Kate had been contemplating death, even planning it, ever since that night in Highgate, yet in the months leading up to her suicide, she had chosen to visit Carolina, to spend some final precious time together. They had stood for almost an hour in front of the Muisca Raft. Carolina was convinced that for Kate – as for the *zipa* – it was a rites of passage, an act of renewal, a cleansing of body and soul. She thought that his daughter had been standing on a threshold, needing to shed her skin. Had she sensed that Kate was feeling suicidal? No. Had her suicide surprised Carolina? No, again.

Suicide was sometimes a spur of the moment, irrational action. However, far more often it was a gradual process, one which began with thoughts, before moving on to plans and finally the act itself. Did it matter what external force had started the entire process? Was there a second murderer behind her self-murder? As sleep took over, a final question: why had Kate not wanted to visit him a final time, to say goodbye?

FIFTEEN

"I nearly mentioned it before your trip to Bogotá, David. My gut instinct was that she must have been sexually assaulted, abused or raped." Lorna Myers was standing in front of the board in Jennings's living room. "Why else would a naturally shy, introverted young woman expose her naked body to a room full of complete strangers? This whole jigsaw is about women's abuse at the hands of men. Judith Shakespeare, Carolina González, Virginia Woolf. Woolf was sexually abused by her two half-brothers as a child, wasn't she?"

"Allegedly, yes. It would certainly explain some of the events in her life and work. But Kate might have been abused as an adult, rather than as a child, Lorna."

"You don't really believe that, do you? What happened in that alley brought back memories hidden away for years. They weren't fresh ones, were they?" Jennings shook his head in agreement. "After you rang last night I looked up a study I vaguely remembered from a few years ago. ACE – the Adverse Childhood Experiences study in San Diego. It set out to show how childhood trauma and abuse have profound, enduring effects on both the mind and the body. It looked at adults' state of health and well-being, and how these are affected by earlier traumatic experiences. What did one expert say?" Myers pulled out a sheet of A4 paper. "That 'the earliest years of infancy and childhood are not lost but, like a child's footprints in wet cement, are often lifelong.' The study found connections between childhood trauma and adult suicide rates. Oh, and women are 50% more likely to have suffered from adverse childhood experiences. I didn't agree with everything in the report, of course. I rarely do." Myers and Jennings shared a smile. "I can understand the causal links between childhood trauma and adult health risk, but 'high-level promiscuity'? Really? I'm not convinced by that."

Jennings's laugh hinted that she wouldn't be. "The study describes suicide as a psychiatric disorder. Well, is suicide itself irrational, or is it the world we live in and the people we encounter who are fucked up? It's men like Craig Tosh and Johnny Holmes who mess women up, David, who send them to the edge. We shouldn't be labelling the act of suicide as *disorder*. Sometimes it is a final attempt to put order back into a damaged life. Nevertheless, I guess the practitioners are right about one thing; everything connects, doesn't it?" Jennings nodded. Most things seemed to. "So where do you go from here?" He surprised himself with the swiftness of his reply.

"Home. Back to Singapore. I think I've gone as far as I can with the investigation. Kate was traumatised, at least twice. She tried to cope: the nude modelling, the trip to Bogotá, communing with writers and characters she admired and who had endured similar experiences. Eventually she decided that life was too brutal."

"The Theatre of Cruelty? Yes, that sounds about right. When are you leaving?"

"I want to spend a few days with Peter. Have a last supper here in Brighton with your good self, Sam, Graham, and Vince. Then I'll be off." Jennings's phone vibrated. He looked at the screen. "Talk of the devil."

****

Jennings was walking along the promenade. The sun was out and there was not a cloud in the sky. No wind either, so no Charlie Chaplin comedy figures on the sea front. Spring was in the air, which had enticed numerous morning walkers. Vince Harrison had rung with an odd, vaguely unsettling piece of news. Marcus Johnson had been reported as 'missing'. He left home late on Sunday evening and had not been seen since, neither at his company's headquarters nor at the house in Hampstead. Sixty hours unaccounted for. His disappearance had even warranted a brief mention on the regional television and radio news. Jennings had tried ringing Anne, both on her landline and mobile number. No reply.

Mentally, he was preparing to return to Singapore. He had even booked his flight. Before that, he had a couple of interviews lined up with directors who had worked on *Man in a Suitcase* and Peter was due to arrive for the weekend. He had left a message with the letting agent to say that he would be leaving at the end of the month. If Graham Miles was right – that our children become strangers to us – then he felt that he had grown closer to Kate during the past few weeks. Had his investigation been a selfless act? No. Had it been a worthwhile mission? Yes. Apart from the burning sense of need – that it was something he *had* to pursue – he had met some incredible people. Courageous, dignified and kind men and women who had shared their experiences with him, opened up a new, dangerous world. He had been closeted in an ivory tower most of his life, while these people had been living in a far more real sense: Sam Gibb, driven to the point of suicide by an evil stalker; Vince Harrison, left to nurse a wife who had given up after their son had hung himself; Graham Miles, who dealt with life and death situations in the course of his daily work; Lorna Myers had found the strength to assert her needs and desires, despite knowing that it would mean leaving her home town and family far behind, for ever; Javier Garcia, dedicated to finding ways to make a difference for people's lives in the *barrio* of Ciudad Bolivar; and Carolina González who had fought back against a pair of feral rapists. He wouldn't forget any of them.

What about Anne, though? Forced to find marital bliss elsewhere, after he had failed to create enough room in his heart for both of his 'girls', she had lost a daughter, and now her husband was missing. Jennings could not simply abandon her for a second time.

****

There was no answer when Jennings rang the Johnson's doorbell. Ten days before, he had been standing in front of a closed front door – at Kate's student flat – waiting to be let in. On that occasion he sensed that the house was empty. This time he instinctively knew that Anne was at home. He rang the bell a second time and stepped back on to the pavement. An almost imperceptible movement of the living room curtain confirmed his suspicion. Seconds later, Anne was almost dragging him in. With the door firmly closed behind them, she embraced him in a bear hug. Jennings was stunned, unsure how to react, or whether to reciprocate. After a few seconds she heaved a sigh, released her grip and apologised.

"I needed that. Oh, and don't get any ideas above your station – it might just as well have been the milkman."

"Charming!"

"Well, maybe I'm exaggerating. It's been a hellish couple of days."

"Any news?"

"None. Mind you, with Imfrax and the press constantly ringing, I'm not answering either of the phones. I'm reliant on e-mails and personal callers."

"Has he done this before? Gone AWOL?"

"He sometimes spends the night at his club in the City. But he always rings, however inebriated he is. No, something's happened."

"How do you mean?"

"I'd been out with a couple of artist friends on Sunday. Just a few drinks and a light supper at Café Rouge. When I got home Marcus was in a strange mood. Nervous. On edge. Smoking in the house – which he never does. He knows how much I hate it. Drinking single malt as if the end of the world was nigh."

"Did you ask him what was wrong?"

"Marcus doesn't function like that. He rarely opens up about personal worries. He has a doctorate in the Stiff Upper Lip. At first I thought that it was an accumulation of all the stress; that he'd cracked under the strain. In the last three weeks we've all been trying to come to terms with Kate's death, but Marcus has been rejected: by the political party he desperately wanted to represent in the House of Commons, and by some of his board at Imfrax. They've launched an internal investigation into allegations about the buying and selling of black market tickets for major sporting events – Wimbledon, cup finals...Some journalists have been hounding him and there's even talk of the Government getting involved."

"You said 'at first'."

"David, you have to promise me something."

"What?"

"That you're not going to fly off the handle." Jennings frowned, puzzled by the demand.

"I'll try."

"Marcus suddenly dragged me into the studio. He asked me if I was accusing him of something. Was I trying to force a confession? Did I want him sent to prison?"

"I don't understand."

"When we met at that café in West Hampstead – you gave me Barry Kenton's painting. Neither of us knew what to do with it, did we? Well, a few days ago I realised that it was ridiculous to keep it hidden away, like some dirty secret. I decided to hang it up in my workshop. It's silly, maybe, but it felt as if she was there, somehow, each time I was painting. Marcus must have gone in there on Sunday while I was out and seen it. He started shouting at me, screaming. Ordered me to burn it. Then he stormed out of the house.

"Why would he react like that, Anne?" Jennings's ex-wife buried her head in her hands. As an unthinkable possibility began to form in his mind, he started to wonder if she had had it buried in the ground for the past ten years. "If I find out that Marcus touched Kate, Anne, I'll kill him! Why didn't you tell me about this, days ago?"

"For Christ's sake, David! What do you think's been going through my mind for the last two and a half days? All the times I was out at exhibitions or retreats, and Marcus was looking after the children. The evenings when I read to Peter in bed, while he read to Kate."

"Do you think he could have abused her?"

"She never said a word."

"What about the self-harming?"

"The specialist thought it might have been because her daddy had gone away. Abandoned her. I never, ever thought it could have meant –" Jennings did not know what to think. He felt nauseous. He had never liked Marcus, but neither had he ever thought of the man as being a potential monster, a child molester, a paedophile. Jesus, it was almost incest. Shouting at Anne wouldn't achieve anything, though. Nor was it fair on her. Had he told her Carolina's story? He had not even told Anne about his trip to Bogotá. It was time to put the record straight, share Kate's story with the woman who had given birth to her and loved her for twenty years. Before that, they needed to agree on the way forward.

"There's only one way of finding out, Anne. We have to ask him. Face to face." Anne was nodding, then sobbing as Jennings held her close. Christ! If Marcus had abused Kate, that also deepened his own sense of guilt. If Marcus was the other killer behind Kate's self-murder, then it made him a culprit too. If only he had found room for Anne and Kate in his affections, she would still be alive. The same questions and regrets swirling around his mind. "Where could he be? What did you tell the police?"

"That he was in an agitated state. That he'd been drinking. That he stormed out the house, without his phone, wallet or car keys."

"Did you mention the painting?" Anne shook her head. Of course she hadn't. What could she have said? 'Oh, officers, there might be a possibility that my husband abused my daughter who, by the way, has recently taken her own life.' Jennings suddenly found his vision blurred – a heady mix of tears and feeling faint. He sat down, allowing the waves of shock, misery and anger to flow over him. He was drowning.

****

Marcus Johnson took one last glance around the first floor living room. Its generous-sized windows looked out over the shingle beach and the North Sea. Anne had never known about the Georgian cottage in Aldeburgh, which had been bought through his offshore company. This was his private hideaway. It was where he came to feed his filthy habit. To think that Anne disapproved of him smoking in the house. What would she make of him if she knew the real truth? Hours spent staring at images of little girls on his laptop. He had tried to justify it thousands of times to himself – that it was better to look than to touch. Of course it didn't wash. People who looked at these girls required others who took the images. It was a food-chain of sick bastards. 'Indecent' hardly touched the surface.

Why had he bought a cottage here? Here being Crag Path, where it had all started. Where his Uncle John had abused him every summer holiday for three years. Tiptoeing into his bedroom in the attic, drunk and stinking of cigars. Why had he never told his parents? Was it his uncle's threats? The fear of not being believed? No. It was the sense of guilt. As if it had been his fault somehow. Had be bought this house in a bid to confront the past? If so, he had failed miserably.

When Anne had moved in with the children he had told himself that everything would be fine. Thousands of men and women are abused as children, yet grow up to be normal people who do not themselves abuse. For the first two years he had thought about Kate, about the possibilities, each time he read to her in bed. But he was in control. He had his photographs to feed off. Then one night, while making love to Anne, he found himself thinking about Kate. A week later he had crept into her room, ignored her pleas for him to stop. It had never happened again. But that one occasion had been once too often. Once had been enough – to mark him as a monster, as bad as Uncle John. Once had been enough – to send Kate to her death eight years later when her mind had digested, fully processed and reviewed her stepfather's betrayal.

At the start of their marriage he had wanted to tell Anne about Uncle John. Nearly had a couple of times when he was drunk. He always stopped himself though. It was like the bullying and the same-sex activity which had been rife in his boarding school. You didn't talk about it; you pretended it had not happened.

He decided to leave the laptop plugged in and running. That way the police, Anne, Peter and David could all see him for what he was

– an animal. Worse than an animal – most of them wouldn't behave as he had. There was a certain symmetry to it: the abused abusing, the killer behind the suicide killing himself. No suicide note. No apologies, excuses or explanations. The secret of Uncle John would go to the bottom of the water with him.

Johnson locked the house, made his way onto the High Street and walked past the little fisherman's cottages, boutiques, delicatessens, and restaurants of this quirky little coastal town. He passed the timber-framed Moot Hall which had once been in the heart of a busy Tudor port, most of which had been lost to the sea. Two of Sir Francis Drake's ships had been built here, the first female British mayor had been appointed in Aldeburgh over a century ago. Johnson had always liked buying fresh fish from the huts along the seashore; he liked the sign which read, 'Any fresher and it would still be in the sea'. Benjamin Britten used to walk along the beach in the afternoon. Johnson thought about the composer as he passed the fifteen foot high sculpture dedicated to him. The Scallop was something you either loved or hated, two interlocking, broken shells with an inscription from *Peter Grimes*: 'I hear those voices that will not be drowned'. Children were encouraged to climb on it, while adults sometimes sat on it while looking out to sea. Approach from the other direction, and its silhouette resembled something completely different – a knight on his horse. Johnson preferred the scallop image. It suited him far better – a slimy creature hiding away in its respectable, opaque shell.

As he neared the hamlet of Thorpeness, the sky was now crepuscular. In half an hour it would be pitch-black. He began to search out larger stones to fill his deep, duffle coat pockets. It was a perverse reversal of his childhood days on the same beach, picking pretty shells, hoping that Uncle John would not visit that night. He had sometimes wondered as he lay in that attic bed, crying silently after his uncle had left, whether his parents might possibly know what happened. Was that possible? He blinked the memory away.

If Aldeburgh was quirky, then Thorpeness was positively bizarre. A sleepy fishing community turned into a private fantasy holiday retreat by a Scottish friend of JM Barrie. At the centre of this never-never land was the Meare, which was where he was heading. An artificial boating lake with little channels, landings and islands dotted about. Uncle John's presence had even managed to ruin this slice of paradise. Johnson could see the bizarre House in the Clouds, a former water tower disguised by its orange and black weatherboarding. The top did indeed look like a little house floating in the sky. He was close by the Meare now. It was barely three feet deep, but that was deep enough for the purpose.

Night had descended by the time Marcus Johnson walked into the water. He remembered Kate telling him about Virginia Woolf's suicide by drowning, having filled her pockets with stones. He had never read any of her books, was not much of a reader at all. He had looked at his stepdaughter as she read out Woolf's final note. Was there any accusation in her storytelling? He had not seen any. Woolf's suicide note had also been a love letter to her husband. Even he had been moved by it. Woolf had talked about her 'terrible disease' – madness. Well, he had one as well, and – like her – was doing what seemed the best thing to do. As he submerged himself in the water, it seemed as if Kate was whispering those words: 'I hear those voices that will not be drowned'.

****

Jennings accepted Anne's offer of a third glass of wine and a bed for the night. They had eaten something he had not tasted in years – old-fashioned cheese on toast. He could not recall the last time they had sat together like this, just the two of them, relaxed and happy in each other's company. It would have been even before either of the children were born. The wine had loosened his inhibitions, and he voiced the thought.

"It was my fault. I simply brushed you aside when Kate was born. She was my little princess and I –"

"It wasn't just you, David. It was me as well. Feeding, nappies, baby classes…It's all consuming. By the time we'd put Kate to bed we were too knackered to even talk."

"We managed to argue, though."

"Arguing doesn't take the same amount of energy. You can argue on an empty tank, or after a sleepless night. Having a civilised conversation requires effort, thought, subtlety, and compromise. Kate wore us out. And she was wilful, bless her. I can remember her deliberately locking me out the house once when I'd gone into the garden for a fag. She even waved at me. Can't have been more than two at the time. She wanted attention and was happy to play us off against each other. I don't remember Peter growing up; I was too busy chasing after the little madam."

"I'm seeing Peter this weekend. You could always come down to Brighton and join us. We could visit Kate's grave together."

"Yes, I'd like that. Marcus won't come back. I can sense it. He's gone. I should never have married him."

"You weren't to know –"

"That's not what I meant. Marcus needed me. You didn't. And I've always resented that. You had your books and your children. Our children. Marcus had millions…and nothing. He was like an overgrown little lost boy. The art exhibitions bored him witless, I could see it in his eyes, but he would follow me along like a faithful dog. At first it was flattering. Then it became boring. That childish need and reliance. In public, at parties, he was gregarious, outgoing. In private he was very different. And we were too different. Nothing in common. He wouldn't even rise to an argument. You and I fought because we are both opinionated, both passionate. We should have fought harder to make it all work."

"I know. I'm truly sorry."

"I said *we*, David. We. It wasn't just you." Jennings nodded in agreement, happy to share out some of the blame. "You know what? I don't even want to know if Marcus…abused our little girl. Knowing won't bring her back. It won't make the world a better, safer place. We will still wake up to news of terrorist attacks, ethnic cleansing, famine…abuse. Do you remember how we used to lie in bed, talking about how we would protect our daughter from the world? Well, you can't hermitically seal them in a bubble. One day they discover for themselves that the world is full of shit. Most people can live with that. Others – often the most strangely sensitive ones – cannot. Maybe it was in Kate's DNA."

"Maybe."

"I was thinking, last night in bed as I tossed and turned, about the last time I went out to the pictures with Kate and Peter. November last year. We went to see that science-fiction film, *Arrival*."

"I loved that film. Found myself crying uncontrollably for the final five minutes."

"We all loved it too. Spent the half hour Tube ride home chatting about it, even arguing about its message. Peter adored it, but didn't like the time dimension aspect. But you know, as a mother sitting there with her daughter, watching another mother who had lost her daughter, I loved the aliens – those wonderfully mysterious heptapods behind their foggy glass – and their mind-blowing concept of life and time. I envied that linguist Louise Banks. Not the 'gift' of being able to see into the future. More the opportunity to make time fluid, look back into the past as if it is now. "That's how I'm trying to see Kate now. In my mind we are driving into college for her GCSE results; it's her first visit to the seaside; she's going to school for the first time; she's riding on a roller-coaster, not sure whether to laugh or cry; she's just passed her driving test; she's been born, and you're holding her while I'm waiting impatiently to cuddle her for the first ever time. In my mind, she can be all of those on the same day. I haven't met any heptapods, but that's the gift I'm trying to teach myself."

Jennings lay his head against Anne's shoulder, and shut his eyes, trying to share her vision.

SIXTEEN

The last few days of Jennings's stay had passed. He would almost miss this tiny flat under the eaves, with its sound of the waves. He could understand why people were drawn to the sea in their retirement. There was something reassuring about the constant beat of the waves, the seagulls' cries, and the view from the shore out to a horizon where ocean met sky. He could think of far worse places to see out the final tides of a human life.

He had made a major life decision. He would be handing in his notice in Singapore and moving back to England. He knew that his budget would not stretch to a Victorian townhouse in leafy Hampstead, overlooking the Heath. However, he had looked round a two bedroom Art Deco flat in the Highgate area. West Hill Court had been designed by the Scottish architect responsible for some of Grand Central station in New York and – more importantly – the legendary East Stand at Highbury in the 1930s. Connections. His beloved football team and his favourite architectural style. It retained the original parquet flooring and the small second bedroom would make a perfect office. The white-rendered block was set back from the road in its own gardens; it would be hard to find a more peaceful location in the city, in his price range anyway. He loved the large, open-plan reception room with its dark grey Crittall steel windows, although the brown walls in the bedroom might have to be changed. In his mind, he had moved in already.

Peter was excited about his father returning 'home', and Anne seemed pleased too. He would be thinking about them tomorrow during his flight, as they attended Marcus Johnson's funeral at the crematorium in Golders Green. Even if he had not been mid-air, he could not have seen himself there. Peter had decided to go to the service. Partly to offer emotional support for his mother. Also, because he had been fond of Marcus and either could not, or would not, wipe all the happy memories from his mind.

10.30 a.m. and Jennings's luggage was already by the door, even though the taxi was not due until noon. He had been like that ever since he could remember. Anxious, almost paranoid, about being late – for a match, stage play, train journey. He would arrive at a football stadium before the gates were even open, at the cinema before the cleaners had been in to vacuum after the previous screening. Fear of missing out. Fear of a mysterious, unknown external force which might delay him *en route*.

Kate's death had forced him to face fears. His anxiety about time were really a fear about other things – death, the ultimate running out of time; but also fear of wasting his life. He felt it now, that his anxiety about time had always been an anxiety about the meaning (or lack of) in his own life. Moving back to London was partly about that. With Peter, he could still make up for lost time. He realised that the move was also, partly, about Anne. They would never be romantically involved again. Neither of them wanted that. However, something had passed between them in the last few days. A deep friendship rekindled.

The doorbell rang. Surely the taxi driver could not share his own bizarre Lateness phobia? He buzzed the visitor up, prepared himself to leave the flat for the last ever time. The knock at the door was a timid one, not that of a mini-cab driver. On opening it he was faced by a woman with a pale, round face and strawberry-blonde hair tied back in a bun. Her skin was almost translucent. She was like a semi-transparent Victorian doll. She held out a tiny hand, reinforcing the impression of a fragile china figurine. She seemed vaguely familiar, although Jennings was convinced that they had never met before. Then it came to him – he recognised her from the photograph on his crime board, which Sam Gibb had taken down the previous afternoon, before they all headed out for their Last Supper. The missing piece of the jigsaw, even if the picture it made up was already formed. The lady introduced herself as Violet Sugden. She seemed unsure about crossing the threshold, particularly once she had seen the luggage. However, Jennings reassured her and welcomed her in. The studio flat had seen a wealth of visitors over the past few weeks. Violet Sugden would be the final one.

"Forgive me for staring at you in the doorway. I was trying to place you. Kate had a photo of the two of you outside a GPs practice." Sugden nodded. "Are you a doctor?"

"No, no. Nothing as grand as that. There's a little annexe round the back of the surgery. I run a drop-in centre there for female victims of domestic violence. And children. Like Refuge, the mission is to empower them and allow them to rebuild their lives. The main difference is that I only work with women who have been sexually abused, rather than battered by their partners." Jennings nodded for her to continue her story. "In the UK, two women a week are killed by either their partner or ex-partner. We have no idea how many women are sexually abused or raped, by a husband, boyfriend or another member of their extended family."

"And Kate came to see you." Sugden nodded. "Did she tell you about her stepfather?"

"Yes. What she told me is confidential but she wanted you to know certain things. Mr Johnson abused her, but he didn't rape her. It only happened once. That was why she self-harmed. She told him that if he ever did it again she would keep a 'diary' of it on her arms – one mark for each 'visit'. It was her way of fighting back. She told me that in her mind she had forgiven him. Then that night-time attack brought the memories flooding back. She kept referring to it as panic waves crashing over her."

"Did you tell the police?"

"That's not how I work. I outlined all the options open to her and the support which we could make available. I also suggested that she came to stay in our safe house for a while, but she refused. She felt that it would be making her a victim. I told her that the safe house isn't just about protection. That we try to change people's lives, not just save them. In the end, she volunteered to help, both at the drop-in centre and at the house."

"Did she talk about suicide?"

"Yes. I told her about all the services and counselling that was available out there – whether it was dealing with either her stepfather's abuse, the alleyway attack, or more generalised fears about men. Then one day I received a small parcel from her. It contained two letters – one for me and one addressed to you. I was only to pass it on to you if her stepfather was either arrested or passed away. Mine wasn't a suicide note. More a thank you letter. Beautifully handwritten in ink. At the end she said that she had made her mind up about the future and asked me to guard the other letter for you. Kate's mother gave me your address, but said that you were heading back to Singapore, so I decided to deliver it personally. She was a very special young woman, someone who left her mark on my life, someone who made a difference to me, so coming down here was the least I could do. Unfortunately, despite my best efforts, some women cannot simply 'move on', relaunch their lives. Suicidal thoughts can drown the other ones out. They can be incredibly powerful. It can be like carrying the weight of the world and simply wanting to be free of it." Violet Sugden stood up and lightly touched his shoulder, before adding, "I feel blessed, privileged to have met her and got to know her."

She made her way out, leaving Jennings clutching the envelope. It felt as if it contained several sheets of paper. He hoped that Kate would not be asking him for forgiveness. His love for her was unconditional, it always had been. Violet had just summed her up in a succinct, moving way. Kate was a very special young woman, someone who had left her mark on his life, someone who would continue to make a difference to him. Coming over here had been the least he could do.

AFTERWORD

Why? started life back in the early 1990s as a treatment for a six hour television drama serial. On the back of a string of successes including *Missing From Home* (1984) which topped the 'National 100' TV ratings twice and *Travelling Man* (1984-85) which attracted a peak viewing figure of over 13 million, Roger Marshall put together a twelve page treatment based around a 'quest':

'*Why?* is a story of a quest...a man's obsessional quest, to discover why his twenty year old daughter found her life so intolerable that she decided to end it.' (*Why?* treatment, p. 1)

He drew on a number of statistics from the time:

'Each year in Britain 5,000 people commit suicide. That's about one every two hours. Put another way, it's about the same total as are killed in motor accidents.' (*Why?*, p. 1)

The parallel is a striking one but – twenty-five years on – is now out of date. In 2014, according to UK Department of Transport figures, 1,775 people were killed on our roads, compared to 5,217 back in 1990. However, the figure for UK suicides had risen to 6,122, with female suicide rates in England at their highest for a decade. [1] In other words, you are (almost) three and a half times more likely to take your own life than lose it in a road accident. This leads me to conclude, sadly, that while great strides have been made in recent decades to improve road safety – through both changes in the law and public awareness, as well as technology – little seems to have been achieved in terms of suicide. This despite the work put in by The Samaritans and other organisations to increase awareness, reduce the stigma, encourage people to seek help before they reach crisis point, and provide accessible support and services. [2] More people are deciding that life is no longer worth living and are taking that 'final desperate refuge from a world that has become intolerable', as one newspaper article from the 1990s put it. Roger Marshall was aware of the irony of the anachronistic term 'commit suicide':

'Until 1961 this uniquely human act was illegal. Survivors woke up to find a policeman by their bed and themselves liable to criminal prosecution'. (*Why?*, p. 2)

He was interested in tackling what he felt was 'still a fiercely controversial issue', suicide still considered by many to be 'anti-social' and 'a sin against God'. He felt it was a topic which 'haunts' many of us and 'has touched, however obliquely, the lives of most. They've either known someone, heard of someone, or read of someone' who took or attempted to take their own life. (*Why?*, p. 1) His research included collating newspaper articles of the time and I was particularly struck by one: '**SUICIDE: THE TERRIBLE ESCAPE**', where the journalist observed that, however shocking the statistics are, the ripple effect is far more disturbing: 'We see the Home Office figures, but the suffering that produces them is beyond measure.'

While in Europe it is men over seventy who are most likely to kill themselves, Roger was particularly interested in why a seemingly well-balanced, intelligent young woman – with her life mostly ahead of her – might take her own life. Looking through the clippings, another headline struck me: '**ONE IN TEN GIRLS TRIES TO KILL HERSELF**'. Another one reflected how little we really know about what goes on inside a loved one's mind: '**In the 26 days since she's vanished, I've learned more about my daughter than I bothered to find out in 20 years**'. It was this elegiac headline which seemed to point towards my father's interest in an ordinary man turning detective:

'He is a forty-five year old businessman. Not being a cop, he knows no more about the Law and Criminal Procedure than the rest of us.

Nevertheless, in our story, he is the Investigator. He asks the questions and ferrets for the truth. It is his struggle, his compulsion to know...the clue by clue detective story... that forms our basic storyline.' (*Why?*, p. 3)

My father wanted to explore the 'powerful' link between a man (David) and his dead daughter (Kate), a father unable or unwilling to accept that she 'chose death in preference to a life that no longer made sense.' (*Why?*, p. 6)

Why? was never commissioned, despite actor John Thaw's interest in teaming up with Roger once again, as they had done for *Redcap* (1966), *What Became of Me?* (1972), *The Sweeney* (1975-78), *Where Is Betty Buchus?* (1982) and *Mitch* (1984). The treatment sat on the shelves in my father's study, gathering dust for twenty-five years. Perhaps both the subject and its dramatic treatment were deemed to be too disturbing. However, the emotive subject of suicide cannot be dismissed or swept under the proverbial carpet. It is the tenth leading cause of death worldwide. Whether or not the self-killer leaves a note – and the majority do not – the act leaves more questions than answers.

Suicide is an act that often asks to be read; it leaves a puzzle as well as a residue of pain. Different cultures and individuals read it in contrasting, conflicting ways: a criminal, sinful or morally wrong act; a form of protest; the ultimate expression of either cowardice or bravery; a reflection of hopelessness; the ultimate escape from a wicked world. Suicide is sometimes portrayed by the media or in fictional drama as an impulsive act, but it is usually premeditated and planned, leading us to ask whether 'rational suicide' exists.

A number of iconic world landmarks have become infamous as suicide sites. At some of these, barriers have been put in place to prevent suicide attempts. I am thinking in particular of the award-winning Luminous Veil, constructed for Toronto's Bloor Street

Viaduct. It has been 'effective' in preventing people from jumping to their deaths – and endangering the lives of others below – but suicide rates by jumping in Toronto have not decreased since its erection. By taking away a means, you do not take away the desire or need. In *Why?* Kate Jennings does not jump, instead ending her life at a natural beauty spot. However, on one level, David Jennings's compulsion or obsession after his daughter's death is to rip apart a metaphorical, emotional safety barrier, a Luminous Veil. He wants to expose the truth behind Kate's death, no matter what dangers or suffering this will lead to, for him, his ex-wife, or anyone else who loved her.

Back in the 1990s my father was 'mindful of television copyists' and was determined to avoid any on-screen 'instructive' scenes. 'There will be no pill-stuffing sequence.' (*Why?*, p. 12). Of course, copycat suicide is not an exclusively modern phenomena, nor is it limited to television and cinema. Sometimes known as the 'Werther effect', after the doomed protagonist in Goethe's 1770s cult novel, similar controversy nowadays surrounds online sites which offer advice on how to take one's own life. Do these represent genuinely helpful virtual places for those who have made their mind up to leave this world? Or do they simply encourage vulnerable people to kill themselves, reinforcing the romanticized image of suicide which some young people hold? Certainly, in the pre-internet days when my father was writing, he felt a moral obligation to avoid the Werther effect and I have attempted to stay faithful to this in the novel. I have, however, made changes. Originally, the protagonist's name was David Vernon, but I wanted to avoid a surname which can also be a first name. Jennings is now an academic, rather than a businessman. Some other characters have either disappeared or been invented, and I have dragged the story into a contemporary setting, rather than create a period piece. Suicide, paradoxically, is both context-dependent and timeless. That is one of the many reasons why I felt compelled to complete Jennings's story, after my father began it so long ago.

My father had in mind 'a tight time span. The action should occupy approximately two weeks'. (*Why?*, p. 12) I have almost kept to this. In terms of the working title *Why?*, I always liked its simplicity and directness. After all, this is not a straightforward whodunit?, despite the story's use of the detective novel formula. 'Why?' is nearly always a more interesting and complex question, whatever the subject matter. There is not always a clear-cut answer. Even if we can piece together the jigsaw puzzle of a dead person's last actions and some of their final thought processes, revealing the truth does not always bring closure. Sometimes it merely provides us with more questions.

Rodney Marshall
Suffolk, UK
December, 2016

1. Samaritans Suicide Statistics Report 2016, samaritans.org.
2. Samaritans Suicide Statistics Report 2016, samaritans.org.

MAIN CHARACTER LIST

Kate Jennings: twenty year old student
David Jennings: lecturer in Singapore; Kate's father
Anne Johnson: artist; Kate's mother
DI Graham Miles: Sussex-based policeman
Marcus Johnson: millionaire businessman
Peter Jennings: archaeology student; Kate's brother
Sam Gibb: Inquiry Agent
Vince Harrison: investigative journalist
Andrew White: Kate's landlord
Richard Hastings: lecturer in London
Craig Tosh: internet businessman; stalker
Malcolm Peters: builder
Jason Peters: builder
Lorna Myers: American profiler and crime fiction novelist
Barry Kenton: artist
Sara Kenton: artist
Margery Henderson: student admin
Colin Simmons: student admin
Carlos Rojas: Bogotá taxi driver
Javier Garcia: Urbanology expert in Bogotá
Maria González: Carolina's grandmother
Jorge González: Carolina's great uncle
Carolina González: Kate's university friend
Johnny Holmes: bar fly; rapist
Ukrainian: Holmes's sidekick
Violet Sugden: runs a safe house for women

ACKNOWLEDGEMENTS & DISCLAIMER

I made extensive use of the internet during my research for this book, including searches for factual information about historical and literary figures, places, buildings etc. I would like to thank all the individuals and organisations concerned for making this information publically available.

Particular gratitude must go to Matias Sendoa Echanove, for his research into the Ciudad Bolivar settlements on the outskirts of Bogotá (*Bogotá at the Edge: Planning the Barrios*, 2004). I would also like to acknowledge the usefulness of Alex Shoumatoff's February 2009 *Vanity Fair* article, *The Mystery Suicides of Bridgend County* and Cambridge Medicine's 2010 study, *The Impact of Early Life Trauma on Health and Disease: The Hidden* Epidemic. Special thanks to Janet Street-Porter for her *Voices* article in the *Independent* newspaper on 5th August 2016 and to The Samaritans, Refuge, the NHS, Rape Crisis England and Wales, and *Current Archaeology*.

Why? is a work of fiction. Names, characters, businesses, places, events and incidents are either the products of the author's imagination or used in a fictitious manner.